The Lovecraft Coven

THE LOVECRAFT COVEN

Donald Tyson

Hippocampus Press

New York

Sincere thanks to S. T. Joshi, without whom this book would not have been published.

Published by Hippocampus Press
P.O. Box 641, New York, NY 10156.
http://www.hippocampuspress.com

Cover art by © 2014 by Robert H. Knox.
Cover design by Barbara Briggs Silbert.
Hippocampus Press logo designed by Anastasia Damianakos.

First Edition
1 3 5 7 9 8 6 4 2
ISBN13: 978-1-61498-085-8

Contents

The Lovecraft Coven...7

Iron Chain 133

The Lovecraft Coven

1.

Screams woke him from dreamless sleep. He blinked to get rid of the scratchy dryness in his eyes and squinted against the cold light that came through a small barred window opposite the foot of his bed. Through the window he saw naked branches of a treetop moving like skeletal fingers against a leaden overcast. His gaze wandered to a grey shadow in an upper corner of the room. Cobwebs, lots of them. There was something drawn on the white walls, lines of some kind, but his eyes refused to focus on them. He closed his eyelids.

When he opened them again, his mind was clearer. He struggled to sit up, and only then realized that he was bound into some kind of grey canvas restraint and strapped to his bed, which he saw was no more than a narrow cot of painted cast iron. It squeaked when he lurched against the straps. The screams continued intermittently. They were some distance away and muted by intervening walls. He twisted his neck and saw that the door to his room was plated with steel, and painted the same dull white as the walls and the bed frame. Everything in the room was white or grey.

No, not room, he corrected himself—cell. He lay on his back strapped to an iron cot in some kind of prison cell. Listening, he heard the distant clang of a sliding steel door slammed shut, and the mutter of a male voice issuing an order of some kind. He could not quite distinguish the words about the screams.

"Will you shut up, you crazy bastard. Shut up! Shut up! Shut up!"

The angry words came from some distance beyond the steel door, presumably from further down a corridor. The screams stopped for several heartbeats, then resumed.

He returned his attention to the walls of his cell. Someone had covered them with the bold black lines of a charcoal drawing stick, or perhaps a black crayon, he could not tell which. Some of it was words in a variety of different scripts. He recognized the Tetragrammaton in four Hebrew letters, and the Greek letters of the name of God, *Deus*. There was writing in another script, some sort of occult alphabet, that he did not know.

In addition to the words, occult symbols covered the walls, in places overlapping so thickly that there was more black than white. The eye in the triangle. The pentagram. Signs of the zodiac. Alchemical symbols. Geomantic figures. He noticed the looped crescents that represented *Caput Draconis* and *Cauda Draconis*, the Head and the Tail of the Dragon, a figure used in ancient astrology. Various other symbols that appeared to be spirit sigils were scattered here and there.

Longer straight lines and sweeping curved lines crossed through the sigils and pentacles. He followed them with his eyes, and found that they converged in the upper corner where the cobwebs gathered. Or were they spider webs? They seemed to be uncommonly numerous and dense. He could not quite see the corner of the room through their occlusion. As he stared at their shadow, it seemed to darken, and to move.

Blinking, he looked away and licked his lips. They were dry and rough against the tip of his tongue. He realized that he was thirsty. How long was it since he had last had a cup of tea? Or even a drink of water? He tried to swallow the dryness, and it got caught in the back of his throat and made him gag. He coughed and worked his tongue around in his mouth to gather saliva, and swallowed again, this time with greater success. His head felt oddly hollow, and he wondered if he had been given drugs.

How had he come to be in this cell, strapped to this cot in what could only be called a straitjacket? Had he suffered some accident? A head injury, perhaps? When he moved his head on the unyielding mattress of the cot he detected no bandage, nor was there any trace of pain other than a mild throbbing between his eyebrows. Had there been a bruise or a wound, he would have felt it. Then what? A fit of some sort? Another possibility occurred to him but he pressed it firmly back into the depths of his mind. He was not ready to consider that possibility quite yet.

Like a persistent wasp, the thought returned. His father had gone mad while he was a young boy, and been locked away in Butler Hospital. Not many years ago his mother had joined her late husband in madness and had died in the same venerable institution for the insane. He had always dreaded the loss of his reason. To consider the wonders of the natural world, the motions of the stars in their heavens, the geology of the terrestrial globe, logically in the strict terms of science, was everything. Without reason, life would not be worth living.

Was it possible that he had gone raving mad, just like his father? Had the authorities been forced to restrain him? A more terrible thought came into his mind. Had he hurt some other human being in his madness? Was this an asylum for the criminally insane?

His last impression before waking in this cell was of lying down in his hospital bed to go to sleep. With a kind of mental jolt, he remembered his cancer. How could he have forgotten it, even for an instant? The doctors had told him it was too advanced to be removed by surgery. He had only weeks to live, or perhaps only days. They had taken him from his house at sixty-six College Street to Jane Brown Memorial Hospital to die.

Very gently, he tensed the muscles of his lower abdomen. There was no pain, not even a trace of it. He tried again, jerking his stomach muscles in a way that always produced a stabbing knife of agony. Nothing. For the first time in more than a month, the pain was gone. Not just gone, but gone so completely that it was hard to remember how it had felt.

Movement in the upper corner of the room drew his attention. He squinted into the shadows. Something shifted behind the screen of spider webs, if that was what they were. Now that he looked at the shadow, it appeared too uniform to be made up of webs of any kind. Whatever moved behind it was too big to be an insect. The air around the shadow had a kind of shimmer that only revealed itself at the corners of his vision. When he looked directly at the shadow, the shimmer could not be noticed, but when he looked half-away, he saw it dance at the edge of his sight.

Above the screams that never entirely ceased, he heard a very faint music. It had the ethnic flavour of the Middle East, and consisted of reed flutes of some sort accompanied by the plucked strings of an unfamiliar instrument similar in tone to a mandolin. It was so faint, it was almost like the sound of a buzzing fly entangled in a spider's web. As he lay listening with his attention on the music, it became easier to hear. There was something hypnotic about it. Fantastic images began to arise in his mind.

The harsh clang of a large steel bolt driven back into its retaining bracket broke his concentration. He flinched and blinked rapidly several times. The door of his cell squealed open.

2.

A big man in a white coat entered pushing a wheelchair in front of him. He had a beefy, butcher-boy face and brick red hair that was buzzed close to his scalp so that it stood straight up like the nap of an Oriental carpet. His eyes were a surprisingly attractive nut-brown, their gentleness in contrast to the broken bridge of his nose, which had been inexpertly set many years ago and bent toward his left cheek a noticeable degree.

"How are you feeling today, Mr. Willifred? Awake again? That's good, that's good."

The man in the straitjacket regarded in silence for several seconds the hulking figure that bent over his cot.

"What was it you called me?"

The attendant stopped and stared down at him.

"What I always call you. What's wrong with Mr. Willifred? Do you want me to call you something else?"

"My name is not Willifred," the reclining man said, enunciating his words with careful precision. "My name is Lovecraft. Howard Phillips Lovecraft."

The attendant looked at him blankly, then grinned and chuckled. He was missing one of his upper front teeth.

"*The* H. P. Lovecraft? The writer?"

The man who called himself Lovecraft frowned.

"As it happens, I am a writer, though I don't see what that has to do with anything."

The attendant began to unbuckle the restraints that held him to the cot, still chuckling.

"I never know what you're going to say next, Mr. Willifred. Before it was all that talk about elder gods and soul-hunters and other dimensions, and now it's Lovecraft. You're a riot."

Lovecraft allowed the attendant to help him into a sitting position on the side of the cot.

"What is your name?"

The attendant chuckled again and shook his head.

"Same as it's always been, Mr. Willifred."

"Humour me for a moment, please."

"It's Chuck. Chuck Spivack, just like always." The amusement in his voice was replaced by a hint of annoyance. "Don't give me any trouble, I don't like to get physical with you."

"Would you please tell me where I am, Mr. Spivack?"

"You're not kidding me?" Spivack peered into Lovecraft's eyes. "If you're serious, I'm going to have to inform Doctor Suskind. He'll want to know about it. We're supposed to report any change in your condition."

He put his hand under Lovecraft's hip and half-lifted the smaller man into the wheelchair. It had a strap dangling from its back that he drew across Lovecraft's chest and tightened.

"Aren't you going to take off this jacket?"

"No can do, Mr. Willifred. Not until we know your episode is over."

"I take it I am in a mental institution. Is it the one in Providence?" He shuddered and forced himself to speak the name. "Is it Butler Hospital?"

"Where else would it be? Now shush your foolishness."

"Where are you taking me?"

"Doctor Suskind gave orders that you were to be wheeled into the common room if you were lucid when you woke up. The way you're talking, I'm not sure but what I should leave you strapped to your bed."

He took grey foam slippers from his coat pocket and slid them on-to the seated man's bare feet. They matched the color of his pyjama bottoms. Lovecraft silently allowed Spivack to finish placing his feet on the steps of the chair and wheel him out of the cell. He glanced back through the open door at the shadow in the corner, but there was no sign of movement. He wondered if he had merely imagined it.

The common room lay on the same level of the hospital, at the end of an L-shaped corridor. Music played gently in the background. He listened for a moment and recognized Mozart.

Spivack pushed him near one of the tall windows that lined one wall of the room. They were protected by heavy wire screens. A big woman in a nurse's uniform sat behind a desk at the end of the room, which was otherwise filled with tables and chairs. The furniture was occupied in a scattered way by about two dozen men and women, who stood or sat in various places. Most of the faces were blank and drooling from excessive medication, but in a few eyes there lurked a manic intensity of focus, even though they stared at nothing.

Lovecraft's attention was distracted by a flickering panel attached to a small wooden platform high on one wall, out of the reach of even the tallest of the men. He looked at it in amazement. It was like a Technicolor cinema screen in miniature. On it, human-sized puppets wearing brightly-coloured fur interacted on the side of a grassy knoll.

He saw that a rubber-coated wire trailed from the back of the panel to a plug on the wall. It was electrical in nature. Several years ago he had attended a scientific demonstration of a similar electrical device, but the crude test image had been colorless, and much smaller. The engineer giving the demonstration had called the process television.

For many minutes he watched the screen with rapt attention, astonished at its brightness and clarity. It was like a tiny window that opened on a stage set where a play was in progress. None of the other inmates appeared to have the slightest interest in the electrical window.

He turned and gazed through the wire screen of the actual window near his chair. It must face the rear of the hospital, he realized, for he found himself looking down from the second floor across a flower garden with gravel walkways and shade trees. The branches of the trees were mostly bare of leaves, which had fallen to the grass, and few flowers bloomed in their beds, indicating a late season of the year. When he had entered Brown Hospital for his cancer, it had been early spring. He noticed on the far side of this little park several smaller buildings of red brick.

His eyes were distracted by the lurid colors on a tattered magazine that lay on a table beside his chair. *Popular Mechanics*. The cover was brighter than he remembered, but then, he had not subscribed for a number of years. It showed some absurd futuristic flying device that was disk-shaped, with no wings and no propellers to drive it through the air. Lovecraft snorted in derision. The editors of the magazine liked to titillate a gullible public by presenting implausible conjectured machines which, they claimed, we would one day use for our conveyance. It was just a way to sell magazines, and sometimes a source of mild amusement, but the articles were never to be taken seriously. No propellers!

It was at that moment in his rambling train of thought that he saw the date on the cover. March, 2013. A kind of vertigo passed through him, and had he not been strapped to the chair, he would have fallen forward. He very nearly lost consciousness.

The date was seventy-six years in the future.

He stared at it, his mind locked. The first thought that came to him, when his brain began to work again, was that someone was playing an elaborate and very cruel practical joke. They had drugged him, taken him out of his hospital room, and were subjecting him to this ongoing abuse. They must be watching him right now.

He looked around the room. The nurse at the desk was deep in reading a small book with flexible paper covers. None of the patients seemed interested in him. A few sketched or coloured pictures at the tables. Two of the older men played chess in the corner, looking like scarecrows propped in their chairs. An overweight woman with skin the color of unbaked bread stood leaning against the wall talking to herself in a low voice while she wagged her head back and forth rhythmically.

How much time passed, Lovecraft would have had difficulty saying. An hour, or perhaps it was two. His mind shut down during this period, and it was only when Spivack returned that he came back into himself and realized that any time had passed at all.

The attendant undid the strap across his chest.

"Doctor Suskind wants to talk to you in his office. He told me to take off your jacket. You better behave yourself, Mr. Willifred, or I'll put you right back in it, and you know I will do it."

With well-schooled fingers he unbuckled the strait jacket and pulled it over Lovecraft's head. Lovecraft worked his arms to loosen up his shoulders. He saw that the cotton top of his institutional uniform matched the grey of his pants.

"Mr. Spivack, would you do me an enormous favour?"

Spivack grunted.

"Depends on what it is."

"Would you get me a glass of water?"

The attendant looked at Lovecraft's dry lips and shrugged.

"Sure. You wait here. Don't get out of this chair until I come back."

Lovecraft watched him leave through the swinging door and stood up. His legs felt weak and stiff. He walked across the room to the nurse's desk, using the tables and chairs for support. The lurid cover of her book bore a picture of a savage dog with its fangs bared, and the enigmatic word *Cujo*. The nurse glanced up with bored eyes.

"Step away from the desk. You know the rules."

"May I just have a quick look at your desk calendar? It won't take more than a moment."

"Step back from the desk."

Her hand hovered above a buzzer that was screwed into the oak desktop. The buzzer had a single large red button.

Lovecraft lowered his eyes and complied. He still felt dizzy, and put his hand on the wall to steady himself.

"You don't listen so good, do you?"

Spivack laid a heavy hand on his shoulder and pulled him around.

"I told you, don't leave the chair. Here's your water. Hurry up and drink it, Doctor Suskind's waiting for us."

He had only asked for water to get Spivack out of the room, but when he started to drink he realized how thirsty he was and finished the glass without stopping.

"Great. Now let's go."

"One more thing. I need to urinate."

"Oh, for the sake of Christ." Spivack rolled his eyes. "OK, we'll visit the john on the way."

The men's room was next door to the common room. When they entered, it was empty. Lovecraft glanced around and made for one of the stalls.

"I thought you said you needed to pee."

"So I do, but not in public."

"Well, aren't you the shy one."

Lovecraft closed the door on the stall and held the walls to keep

15

from falling. He found that his arms shook from the physical reaction to what he had learned. Was it possible that nearly eight decades had passed? Or was he going completely mad, as he had always feared would happen sooner or later? The latter option seemed much more plausible.

He found the lever that flushed the toilet and emerged from the stall.

"Hey, your face is really white. Are you sick or something?"

"No, not sick."

"Well let's go then. Shake a leg."

Lovecraft ignored him and moved toward the sinks.

"I need to wash my hands."

"Then wash them, for the sake of Christ."

It was not until he stood in front of one of the white porcelain sinks that his distracted mind focused on the reflection in the mirror. He stood still and gripped the edge of the sink with all the strength in his hands, staring at his image.

The oval face in the mirror was that of a man around twenty-five years of age, with curling sand-coloured hair. The hazel-green eyes that regarded him were frank and open, concealing no secrets. A thin scar ran through the end of his left eyebrow, the result of some childhood injury. His lips were full and just red enough in their color to lead someone with unkind intentions to call them effeminate. All in all, it was a sincere face, an honest face, a perfectly good face.

But it was not his face.

3.

Doctor Suskind greeted Lovecraft with a warm handshake across his desk and a familiar manner that said they were old friends. He was a narrow-shouldered man of around sixty years who wore a faded green cardigan sweater that smelled of pipe tobacco. Light from the two windows behind him reflected from his oily scalp through thinning grey hair that was brushed straight back from his forehead. As he talked, he wagged his head, which caused the gleam to move back and forth, back and forth, across the top of his skull.

"Take a chair, Monty. Or should I start calling you Howard? Yes, that one is fine."

He motioned Spivack out of his office with backward paddling motions of his hands, and the attendant shut the door quietly after him.

The leather-covered armchair chosen by Lovecraft faced the antique mahogany desk. He glanced across it out the windows. The office was at the other side of the flower garden, on the second level of one of the small brick buildings he had seen from the recreation room. The grey sky and the lateness of the year gave the garden a bleak look.

"May I call you Howard?"

"It makes little difference what you call me, since you won't believe a word I say."

The psychiatrist tut-tutted in his swivel desk chair.

"There's no need for negativity. I'm not here to judge, but to listen."

A brown file folder lay opened across the leather desk blotter. He glanced down at it and spread the papers it contained with his fingertips.

"Would that be my file?"

Suskind hunched his narrow shoulders inside his sweater.

"That's right."

"May I read it?"

"I'm afraid that wouldn't be proper procedure, Howard. There are notations in here that are meant for my eyes only. You might misinterpret them."

"Will you at least answer my questions?"

Suskind smiled vaguely.

"I have an idea. Let's trade questions. You ask one and I'll answer, then I'll ask one and you answer."

The wall beside the desk was lined floor to ceiling with book shelves, all of them filled with books. Lovecraft wondered how many Suskind had found time to read.

"What is . . . what *was* my name?"

"Montague Berkley Willifred." The psychiatrist paused and waited for a reaction. "Does the name mean nothing at all to you?"

Lovecraft shook his head.

"Nothing at all."

It was not entirely the truth. The name awoke some distant echo of memory. But when he tried to bring it into the light, it eluded him.

"Now it's my turn. How long have you believed yourself to be Howard Phillips Lovecraft?"

"All my life."

The psychiatrist raised thin grey eyebrows. Lovecraft shrugged.

"I awoke in one of your cells this morning. For all I know, I'm still asleep and this is nothing more than a bad dream."

"Do you often have bad dreams, Howard?"

"It's my turn, Doctor. Why was Monty Willifred placed into an insane asylum?"

"You—that is to say, *he* had a mental breakdown and killed two young men who were living with him at his house."

"How did he kill them?"

"With a chef's knife from the kitchen."

Lovecraft digested this information. It was worse than he had imagined. If he truly was Monty Willifred, he was not only crazy, but a homicidal maniac.

"Do you remember nothing about the incident? Nothing about your former life?"

He shook his head.

"Why was I in a straitjacket?"

Suskind took a pipe from a rack on his desk and began to load its briar bowl with shredded tobacco.

"That was for your own protection, to prevent you from injuring yourself. Three days ago you became violent and began to rave. You had to be restrained and sedated."

"What did I rave about?"

The narrow little man stopped and eyed him keenly.

"You really don't remember any of it?"

"No."

"It was mostly incoherent. You kept screaming about someone called Narl-something. Narltapoleth. Narlapotep."

Lovecraft flinched at the name and felt his body tremble, but tried not to show it.

"Nyarlathotep."

"Yes, that's it. So you do remember."

"I told you that I recall nothing before this morning. Nyarlathotep is a character in some of my fiction."

The psychiatrist stopped tamping the tobacco into his pipe and picked up a pen to make a note on one of the pages.

"That's interesting. That's very interesting."

"What else did I say?"

"You said something about night-walkers or shadow-walkers." He shuffled through the papers in the file and nodded. "Yes, shadow-walkers. You were afraid that they had broken through, as you put it, and were coming to abduct you."

"Did I say what these shadow-walkers look like?"

"Not directly. You talked a lot about shadow people, old gods, cipher keys, and something called the angular transit of the lunar nodes, whatever that may be."

"All this means nothing to me."

Suskind struck a wooden kitchen match alight on a stone paperweight and puffed the flame into the bowl of his pipe. The rich smell of tobacco smoke filled the air. He began to discuss details of Willifred's medication and therapy. His voice had a droning quality.

Lovecraft gazed past his shoulders through the windows. The grass in the garden was spotted with fallen leaves. They had not yet lost their colors, but looked washed out under the leaden sky.

Something moved beneath the trees, a gliding darkness on the grass. Lovecraft narrowed his eyes. It seemed to gather itself behind the trunk of a weeping willow. The drooping branches of the tree, with their small yellowed leaves, rippled in the breeze like a grass curtain, obscuring and revealing the trunk. He waited, attention fixed on the willow, but the shadow did not emerge. He realized that Suskind was still talking.

"—as paradoxical as it may seem, I find the events of the past several days encouraging. They indicate a transformation in your mental condition, and where there is change, there exists the possibility of improvement. Today I find you one hundred percent improved. You are rational, you are coherent. Your paranoia has abated. Yes, it is very encouraging, Monty, or Howard if you prefer."

"You don't believe I really think I'm Howard Phillips Lovecraft, do you, Doctor? You think I'm pretending."

"At this stage in your treatment, it doesn't matter what I believe. You yourself must come to terms with your past, with who you are and what you have done. A flight into fantasy may offer some temporary relief, but in the long run it is not a practical solution. It's my job to help you confront reality. Think of me as a kind of mirror."

"I suppose it was too much to hope that you would believe. Let me ask you this, Doctor—what is today's date?"

Suskind took his pipe from his lips and regarded Lovecraft with bright eyes for several seconds.

"October the twenty-seventh."

"No, I mean the full date. What year?"

"Oh, I see what you mean. It is the twenty-seventh of October in the year twenty-thirteen."

Lovecraft did the mental arithmetic.

"Yesterday, for me, it was the year nineteen-thirty-seven. Seventy-six years have passed. I find myself thrown into the future, and into the body of another man."

"How does that make you feel?"

"It is disconcerting, to say the very least. Frightening—terrifying, even. But at the same time, it holds a strange fascination. How many men have the opportunity to glimpse the future that lies beyond their mortal term of life?"

Suskind spread his tobacco-stained fingers.

"Until today, I would have said nobody."

Lovecraft chuckled dryly. His new voice still sounded strange in his ears. It was lighter than his old voice.

"And you would still say nobody, to anyone other than me."

The psychiatrist smiled politely. He slid the sleeve of his white shirt back from his left wrist and regarded his watch.

"It's almost visiting hour. I won't keep you any longer today, Howard. You're probably anxious to speak with Janice. She came to the hospital every day this week, you know, even the days when you were sedated. We couldn't keep her away."

Lovecraft denied Suskind the expected response. He merely turned his head to look out the window at the rippling boughs of the willow on the far side of the garden. Something moved behind the screen of yellow leaves, something dark, a shadow on a sunless day.

4.

The young woman in the small private visitor's room did not wait for him to speak. The instant she saw him in the open doorway, she leapt to her feet and rushed to embrace him, covering his face with her fervent kisses and fluttering her fingertips over his cheeks and brow. When she drew away from him, there were tears in her dark eyes.

"Monty, dear Monty, I thought you were lost to me."

The overweight nurse who had escorted him to the room patted her on the shoulder to get her attention.

"I'm right outside the door, hon. If he acts up just give a shout and I'll be in here in two seconds."

She smiled at Lovecraft knowingly and shut the door behind her.

The young woman drew him further into the room and hugged him. He felt the points of her small breasts through the thin grey cotton of the institution uniform he wore. Gently, he grasped her upper arms and held her away to study her.

She was in her mid twenties, tall and slender, with black hair that hung over her shoulders in front and behind. He detected a Mediterranean influence in her angular face—Italian, perhaps, or Sicilian—yet she had no trace of an accent. The thin loop of silver through the side of her nostril shocked him more than her black lipstick. When had women begun to pierce their faces with metal wire? he wondered. Even more startling was the streak of bright purple in her hair that ran from her crown past the left side of her face. It matched the purple of her silk blouse. Instead of a skirt she wore black denim pants that hugged the curves of her legs, and black leather boots that rose midway up her calves. A short brown leather jacket hung across the back of her chair. On the table rested a kind of shiny black helmet with a smoked glass visor, and a pair of black leather gloves.

He glanced around the room. Apart from the table and two chairs, it was unfurnished. The small window opposite the door was in some kind of light well and faced a featureless brick wall no more than ten feet away. Like most of the windows in the hospital, it was covered with a heavy steel mesh. No mirror hung on the wall. There did not appear to be any way of eavesdropping on the conversations held in the room.

"My dear woman, please control yourself."

She blinked at his cold tone of voice and stepped back.

"Monty? What's wrong?"

"What did they tell you about my present condition?"

"They said you were conscious and lucid again."

Lovecraft gathered his thoughts. He had no wish to alienate the woman. He needed her to answer his questions.

"Perhaps you should sit down."

He guided her into the chair that bore the leather jacket, and discovered that its legs were bolted securely to the floor. As was the table. She watched him, blinking rapidly, but said nothing.

"When I awoke this morning, I was no longer Montague Berkley Willifred."

"I don't understand. Monty, you're scaring me."

He drew himself up and squared his shoulders.

"I am Howard Phillips Lovecraft, of Providence, Rhode Island."

Her reaction was not among those he anticipated. She nodded, eyes narrowed in thought.

"It makes sense. Monty's consciousness has been under attack for months. Not even the wards we drew up around the house were enough to stop the assaults. When Booker and Finney went insane and Monty had to kill them, I thought he was gone, too, but his identity must have been hiding deep in his own subconscious. Something came to the hospital last night and took him. That created a vacuum and your soul was sucked into his body at the very moment of your death."

Lovecraft stared down at her, and felt a rising indignation.

"That's the most arrant nonsense I've ever listened to."

"No, it makes perfect sense. They've been trying to steal his soul for months."

"Who are they?"

"The shadow-walkers."

A chill covered Lovecraft's heart like a splash of cold water.

"Shadow-walkers, did you say?"

"That's what we call them. Monty sometimes called them the soul-eaters and said they were trying to kidnap him. We didn't know what he was talking about, but he must have guessed what was coming."

Lovecraft remembered his mother, shortly before she was admitted to Butler Hospital, talking about shadow people. They would peek out at her from behind hedges and around the corners of buildings whenever she went out of the house. He had always dismissed such talk as insane.

"Even if what you say were true, why me?"

She laughed.

"Who else would it be? Monty's been obsessed with you for his whole life. He had all your stories and poetry memorized. Our coven has been working for the past two years to find your book. Monty ate, drank, breathed and dreamed you, Mr. Lovecraft. Who else would come into his vacant body?"

Lovecraft stared silently through the window screen at the brick wall. He appeared outwardly serene, but inside he felt like a drowning man in a tempest. Everything he believed was turned upside. There was nothing solid to cling to.

"What do you mean by a coven? A coven of witches?"

She shook her head, her dark eyes watching him keenly.

"We aren't really witches. We don't follow the Gardnerian or Alexandrian traditions, or any other tradition for that matter. We work magic but it isn't the same as witch magic. It's more like necromancy. When Monty formed our occult group he called it the Lovecraft coven. I thought he was just joking around but the name stuck."

"You mentioned my book? Do you mean a book of my stories?"

"No, *the* book. The one and only."

He stared at her. She widened her heavily made-up eyes and nodded.

"Yeah, *that* book. Monty's been obsessed with finding it for over a year."

"But my dear young woman, it does not exist."

"Are you sure about that?"

"I should be sure. I created it."

She shook her head.

"No, you wrote about it. You dreamed about it. You quoted passages of text from it. But you didn't create it, because it already existed."

"That's absurd."

"As absurd as waking up in somebody else's body?"

He returned to the table on unsteady legs and sat down. She reached across it to grasp his hands in hers. He did not try to pull them back.

"All this must be one hell of a shock for you, Howard. I'd say you're holding up pretty well, considering."

"Don't you doubt what I've told you? For all you know I may be Monty Willifred, gone completely insane, who thinks he's Howard Lovecraft. Isn't that the more rational and likely explanation?"

She shook her head.

"Not when you've done what we've done over the past couple of years, and see the things we've seen. I could tell you stories that would curl your toes. It's a miracle that any of us are still alive."

"You mean because of the necromancy?"

"That's what I mean. We worked rituals Aleister Crowley would never have dared. MacGregor Mathers would have run screaming, and Eliphas Levi would probably have fainted. We went all the way, Mr. Lovecraft, and I mean all the way."

"Please, keep calling me Howard."

She nodded with a flash of a smile.

"I should introduce myself. I'm Janice Fallows. I've been living with Monty for almost three years. We hooked up together because we both had an interest in practical magic. Monty was way more advanced than I was, even back then. He's always been ahead of the rest of the coven. He told us what to do and we did it."

Lovecraft chewed his lower lip, wondering what question to ask. There was so many questions, and he needed to know the answers to all of them.

"Why was Monty so interested in my work?"

"He's your great-grandson."

"That's absurd. My wife and I had no children."

"That's what he told me. I can't swear under oath that it's true, but I can swear that Monty believed it."

"But it's absurd."

"Is it? You were a man, Howard. Men have needs. Think back and tell me it's impossible that none of the women you were with became pregnant.

"It's absurd, I tell you. Other than my wife I was never with another wo—"

Her dark eyes widened, and she smiled.

"Who was she?"

"Lavinea Willifred. I remember now. It was the day of the Bristol Fourth of July Celebration. I attended with some relatives and their friends. I drank hard cider, which is something I never do as a general rule. I'm an abolitionist, you see. Lavinea and I went to a hay barn. She kissed me on the lips, and—but it was all over so quickly. I don't even remember what we did. The cider made me dizzy."

"Lavinea Willifred," she said in triumph. "What are the chances of the names being just a coincidence?"

"Even so, it doesn't prove anything."

"Maybe not in a court of law, but we're not in a court of law, Howard."

Lovecraft sat back in his chair, drawing his fingers away from hers. He shook his head in bewilderment.

"This is so overwhelming. What am I to do about any of it?"

"What are *we* going to do? We're in this together, Howard. You, me, and the coven. The shadow-walkers are hunting all of us. Sooner or later we are all going down, unless we work together."

"How do you mean, going down?"

She shrugged.

"Mental breakdown. Drug overdose. Suicide. Sudden fatal accident."

"What can I possibly do?" he repeated. "I'm a prisoner."

She leaned forward and lowered her voice.

"Not for long. I've made arrangements for the door to your cell to be left unlocked tonight. The night guard is going to turn a blind eye when you go past him and out the side door. That will be unlocked as well. I'll be waiting for you on the street."

He looked at her with a new appreciation.

"How did you manage such a thing?"

She laughed. He discovered that he liked the sound. It was clear, clean and defiant.

"The Willifreds of Providence are not a poor family. Monty got his share. You can do almost anything if you have enough cash."

"When shall I come to you?"

"It doesn't matter. Let's say around midnight. I'll wait for you all night if I need to."

Looking into her eyes, Lovecraft knew she would do as she said.

5.

He did not associate the shadowed figure astride the motorcycle with Janice Fallows until she blipped the throttle, making the engine growl. He stopped dead on the grass and stared at her, amazed. She flipped up her visor.

"Hurry up," she hissed. "It's not safe for us to be out in the open after dark."

Lovecraft quickened his pace. She shook her head when she saw him in the glow of the streetlight.

"Couldn't you find anything else to wear?"

"No, I could not."

He wore his grey hospital uniform beneath a brown terrycloth bathrobe, and on his bare feet the disposable foam slippers that were the standard footwear for the more closely monitored inmates who were on medication or subject to restraints.

"You're going to be freezing by the time we reach the house. Get on behind me. Put your feet on these pegs and hold on tight."

Before he could think of anything more to say, they were off down the deserted street, flashing past parked automobiles at a rate of speed that made Lovecraft cringe. He had never traveled at such a pace, not even by rail. The throaty roar of the bike and the rush of wind past his ears made talk impossible. He tightened his right hand around his left wrist in front of Janice's waist and tucked his cheek against her leather-covered shoulder.

The night was not particularly cold for the time of year, but within a minute the wind had set its icy daggers into his flesh, and he had to clench his teeth to keep them from chattering. They were racing through the streets of Providence, but the city was so changed he could barely recognize it. Only the occasional landmark that had survived the tide of history assured him that he was in the city that he loved before all others. Soon they left it behind and flew down the open highway.

It seemed to Lovecraft that half an hour had passed, or a bit more, when Janice guided the motorcycle off the main road and along a narrow secondary road that wound its way through the forest. By this time he was so cold, he could barely move, but he managed to turn his head behind to mark the way they had come. One of the widely spaced streetlights they had just flashed past winked into darkness. Then another blinked out, and another, and another.

He watched them go dark one by one along the straight stretch behind them, leaving only a featureless sea of black. They were turning off faster now, the darkness racing closer to the motorcycle as though trying to catch up to them. He leaned his lips nearer to the side of Janice's helmet and shouted against the wind.

"The street lights! Behind us!"

She half-turned her head.

"I know. It's the shadow-walkers. Hold on."

The motorcycle seemed to leap forward like a horse that feels the spur in its side. The roar of its engine turned into a scream of pain. Lovecraft would not have believed it possible to go any faster, but their rate of speed almost doubled. He craned his neck backward, and was relieved to see that the failing streetlights fall away behind them. In minutes they were lost amid the wooded hills.

"You can slow down now."

Either she did not hear his words, or chose to ignore them. It was not for many miles that she backed the throttle, and that was only to guide the motorcycle into an unlit narrow lane. At least it was paved. When the bright beam of the headlamp illuminated the front of a darkened mansion, Lovecraft realized that they had come up a long driveway, and arrived at their destination.

She killed the engine and set the bike on its kickstand, then got off. He tried to follow and discovered that he could not move his legs. Without a word, she helped him to lift one leg over the gas tank and slide off the side of the seat.

"Can you walk?"

"I think so." His teeth chattered. "It's the damned cold."

"You'll be all right when we get inside. Come on, we can't stay out here, it isn't safe."

The front door of the big dark house opened, and a slender young man wearing jeans and a white turtleneck sweater came down the stone stairs. Without a word he took Lovecraft under one arm and Janice took the other. They helped him under the pillared portico and into the mansion.

A wave of warmth washed over him. The house was not dark inside, but only seemed so because of black curtains at all the windows. The muted interior lighting was adequate to show that the man holding his right arm had platinum-blond hair pulled behind his head into a ponytail. He looked Germanic, Lovecraft thought—a typical Aryan type with a long straight nose and a lofty forehead. On one cheek he wore a tattoo in the shape of a red lightening bolt.

They led him from the entrance hall to a sitting room and lowered him onto a couch. Lovecraft was gratified to see that a fire burned in the fireplace. He welcomed the additional warmth, although the house seemed to have a central heating system—he noticed cast-iron radiators against the walls.

Janice pulled off her helmet and gloves. Her cheeks were flushed from the cold air.

"Where are the others?"

"In the ritual room, holding the wards," the young man told her. "It seemed a prudent safeguard, under the circumstances."

She turned to Lovecraft and examined him with a critical eye, then took his thigh between her hands and held it.

"You're freezing. You may have hypothermia. Get him a blanket, Luther."

The blond German, as Lovecraft thought of him, even though he had no trace of an accent, left the sitting room, and in the space of a minute returned with a grey woollen blanket. She wrapped this around Lovecraft's shivering shoulders.

"We were chased on the highway."

"They know he's here by now," Luther said.

His tone was neutral. He might as well have been talking about the weather.

"The new wards will hold."

"What are these wards?" Lovecraft asked, his voice shaking.

Janice and Luther looked at each other.

"He really is gone, then," Luther said.

"I told you so. They must have found a way to bypass his protective sigils while he was asleep."

Luther stared at Lovecraft with serious blue eyes and bent close.

"Are you truly H. P. Lovecraft?"

"I am, unless I've gone completely mad."

He straightened his back.

"This is fucking amazing."

"It can't be an accident. Monty must have planned for this to happen if he was ever taken by the shadow-walkers."

"He never said anything about it to me."

"Nor to me," she agreed. "But it can't be just chance."

"I'll ask again—what are wards?"

"Occult barriers, erected by ritual work to protect places and people from malicious magic."

"You mean to say this house is protected by magic?"

Janice smiled briefly.

"And so are you, now that you are inside it."

Lovecraft thought about this for a moment.

"Didn't the killings take place inside this house?"

Luther nodded.

"We thought we were protected, but the wards failed."

"It won't happen again," she assured him.

They were silent for a time. Janice put more wood on the fire, and Luther went to the window and pulled back the black curtain to peer out through the crack. Very faintly, Lovecraft heard the music of flutes and gently plucked strings. It was similar to what he had heard in the hospital.

"They're all around the house," Luther said.

"Why are they pursuing us?" Lovecraft demanded.

"I told you at the hospital. Monty wants your book, and there is something on the other side—something very powerful—that is determined to prevent us from ever getting it."

"Surely that's over now. With Monty gone, why should you continue your coven?"

"We swore a compact together," Luther said. "I won't betray my oath now that Monty has been taken."

"None of us will. We'll find a way to get him back."

Both turned to look at him. There was no need for them to speak. He knew what they were thinking. If Monty's soul returned to his body, he would be displaced with nowhere to go. His own body had been rotting in Swan Point Cemetery for almost eighty years.

6.

Is this a séance?"

"Something like that," Luther told him. "We'll open a rift between our world and the other side, and try to communicate with Monty's soul."

They sat at a round wooden table in what Janice called the ritual chamber, a spacious room on the second level of the mansion. It was mid-afternoon of the following day. Sunlight streamed through the tall windows at a sharp angle, missing the table but painting the floorboards near the wall with panels of gold.

He had slept in Monty's bed, and now wore Monty's clothes, which were a bit too colourful for his conservative tastes. The body-hugging shirt was paisley, and the too-tight and absurdly low cut pants were lavender corduroy, but at least they fitted. So did his alligator-leather shoes. It would have been foolish to try to borrow clothes from one of the other coven members, when he had an entire wardrobe at his disposal. Even so, Lovecraft could not entirely shake off the sense of wearing the clothing of a dead man. There was something just a bit ghoulish about it.

Luther still had on what he had worn the previous night, leading Lovecraft to wonder if he had slept, but Janice had changed into a loose shirt of unbleached cotton and black leather pants. The other residents of the house were equally casual about their attire. Despite the wide variety of garments, Lovecraft gathered from their materials and cut that they were expensive. The same was true of the bits of jewellery he saw, leading him to conclude that none of Monty's friends was hard up for money.

Over the course of the morning he had discovered that five members of the coven still occupied the mansion along with Janice and Luther, who appeared to be their unofficial leader in Monty's absence. Two of them were young women, the other three equally young men. Three others had fled from the house the night of the killings. No one knew their fate.

He felt old sitting in their company, but then, he had always felt older than others, even while still a young man himself. Someone involved in the pseudo-religion of Theosophy had once told him that he possessed an ancient soul, and that was why he felt himself senior to those around him. At the time, he had made a joke about it, but as he grew older the remark seemed increasingly apt. It was undeniable that some individuals were more mature than others, and their levels of maturity had little to do with their relative ages, or their upbringing for that matter. It was something inherent. Not that he believed in the existence of a soul.

"Before we begin, I should introduce you formally to the other members of the coven. Some you've already run into around the house. From your left side, clockwise around the table, are Meg Levi, Aaron Reed, Steffi Fernwood, Leroy White, Janice you already know, and on her left is Ozzie Gillespie. And there's me—Luther Cargrave."

"Girl-boy, girl-boy, girl-boy," Lovecraft murmured.

"We try to balance the sexual polarity when we work, but as you see we're short on female members."

"Will that make a difference?"

"Probably not. We can compensate to some degree by projecting our energies into the voids created by the imbalance."

"I confess, I'm a bit nervous. I may have written about magic but I've never practiced it."

"After all the things you've written, it's hard to believe you're not a magician," the woman named Meg Levi said. She was a compact little woman with short dark hair and a hard face.

"My aunts would never have countenanced the practice of necromancy in our house," he said with a faint smile. "I had a hard enough time getting them to accept my experiments in chemistry."

"There's no reason to be afraid," Luther assured him. "Trance mediums invoke the souls of the dead on a regular basis with no apparent harm to them."

"I need scarcely point out that I am not a trance medium."

"Our medium today is Steffi."

The curly-haired blond woman three places to his left smiled and nodded.

"She's the best trance medium in the coven—the best we have left, at any rate." Luther said.

"Well thanks," she said in a tone of injured pride and several of the others laughed nervously.

Lovecraft could sense the unease around the table. They were tired, frightened, near the breaking point.

"My friend, Harry Houdini, would be skeptical."

"Just relax, Howard," Janice said. "We'll do all the work. We know what we're doing."

He had the impulse to ask if they had known what they were doing the night two of their fellow coven members had gone insane and tried to murder them, but he held his silence.

Luther lit a small oil lamp that rested in the center of the table, then went to the windows and drew the black drapes, shutting out the sunlight. He turned on an electrical machine on a side table, the function of which Lovecraft could not even guess, until the music of one of Bach's Brandenburg Concertos began to murmur in the background. Lovecraft marvelled at the quality of sound that came out of the device. It was immensely superior to the sound of the spring-driven gramophones with which he had grown up.

Going to a small table against the wall, Luther took a crystal bowl and began walking around the séance table clockwise, muttering under his breath as he went. With each step he reached into the bowl and threw a pinch of its contents across the hardwood floor. It was salt, Lovecraft realized. Luther must be cleansing the room. He watched the coven leader do the same thing with a matching crystal bowl of water, which he sprinkled from his finger tips, and with a bowl that contained a cone of burning rose incense. The sickly-sweet scent filled the air. The third circumambulation completed, he returned to his chair.

"Join hands," he said.

Lovecraft accepted Luther's fingers into his right hand, and Meg Levi's into his left. He had to extend his arms to reach them. The table was large enough to have seated twice as many people. There were substantial gaps between their chairs.

"Concentrate on the flame of the lamp. Remember Monty Willifred. Remember the sound of his voice, his laugh, the clothes he liked to wear, the smell of his aftershave, everything that identifies him in your mind."

They fell silent, their attention focused on the steady flame that rose from the wick of the lamp. The lamp had no glass shade, but the flame never flickered. Lovecraft did not know what image to hold in his mind, so he decided to visualize Monty's bedroom closet. At least it had an association with the man. His strong scepticism for all forms of ritual magic was subdued by the strange circumstances in which he found himself.

Steffi straightened in her chair and took a deep breath. She held it, staring up at the ceiling, then released it with a shudder.

"I feel him," she said in a little girl's voice.

"Ask him where he is," Luther ordered.

"He can't talk. He's a prisoner. I can see his lips moving through the glass but I can't hear what he's saying."

"Can you read his lips?"

She shook her head, her blond curls dancing. Her eyes were squeezed tightly shut.

"I don't know, I don't know."

"Ask what we can do to help him."

"He's speaking slowly, forming words with his lips. Find . . . the book. I think that's what he said. Find the book."

"Ask him what we can do to return him to his body."

Again she shook her head, more violently this time.

"His lips are moving but I can't hear him. His hands are pressed against the glass and he's staring right at me. Danger. That's what he keeps repeating. You're all in danger. Get out, get out, get out."

She groaned and seemed to collapse in upon herself. Only the grasp on her hands kept her from slipping out of her chair. Aaron and Leroy pulled her back up and held her head away from the table. Her wide eyes stared unblinking but she did not see the flame of the lamp, or the faces it illuminated. She saw something terrifying.

"They're coming!" she shrieked in a high-pitched scream.

"Who is coming? Steffi, who is coming?" Luther demanded.

The flame of the lamp elongated itself to an impossible length and began to dance and flutter like a living thing.

"Put it out, quickly," Steffi said. "Now, put it out."

"Release hands," Luther ordered.

Lovecraft heard the atonal piping of reed flutes and the twang of strings. It was the same alien music he had heard at Butler Hospital, but much louder, much stronger.

"Aaron, Leroy, take care of Steffi. Janice, open the curtains. Quickly, before they break through."

He leaned forward and tried to blow out the flame of the lamp, but it only blazed more brightly. Lovecraft stood and backed away from the table. The flame split down its center, forming a dark rift around which its two columns danced. Something dark and thin flashed out of the divided flame. It reminded him of a thin man in a dark suit squeezing through the crack in a closing door at the last instant. Janice cried out in pain. Lovecraft realized that the shadow had knocked her off her feet as she reached for the curtains. He went to her and raised her to her feet.

"The curtains, open the curtains," she muttered, her eyes rolling back beneath her fluttering eyelids.

There was chaos in the room. More of the shadows had managed to squeeze through the flame before Luther doused it with the pitcher of water on the side table, plunging the room into almost total darkness. The shadows had a kind of silver flicker around their edges that rendered them visible against the black. Lovecraft watched one of them force its way into the face of Steffi Fernwood. She seemed to breathe it in like black smoke.

"Keep your mouths closed!" Luther shouted above the growing cacophony. "Cover your nose and ears. Don't look at them."

Leroy White made a dash for the closed door and seized the handle, but the shadows were there ahead of him. They twisted his body as he covered his face with both hands and threw him against a wall. Lovecraft heard several bones snap. He bounced off and fell to the floor like a broken doll.

"We have to get out," Meg Levi yelled.

She began to scream and beat at the darkness above her head. The room was almost pitch black. Only thin slivers of light came through a crack in the window curtains and under the closed door. Lovecraft cradled Janice against his chest and tried to move away from the shadows, which were concentrated most thickly in front of the windows and door, as though to defend them. He realized that they needed the darkness.

"We can't reach the curtains," he told Janice.

"We have to get out of this room," she said.

Her arms tightened around his neck, almost choking him. He half-lifted her away from one of the male coven members, he could not tell which one in the dark, who flailed his arms and struck both the wall and himself indiscriminately.

"They get inside your head," Janice said into his ear, above the curses and howling. "We have to get out of here."

Lovecraft looked desperately around in the darkness. He could no longer see the crack under the door—something obscured it. The light from the gap in the curtains was becoming less intense with each passing second. It was as if the shadows were thickening the darkness. He blinked and squinted. Something glowed dull red on the walls. Lines of some kind. They looked as if they were drawn in weak neon tubes.

"Do you see that?" he asked Janice.

"See what? I don't see anything."

The lines were like the lines in charcoal that Monty had drawn on the walls of his cell. They all angled toward the same corner of the room. He squinted and stared into the place where the lines converged. Something was there. It looked like the crack in a low doorway. He began to draw Janice toward it.

Someone bumped into him and cursed. He recognized Luther's voice and reached out to grasp his arm. The other man flailed against his touch but at least realized that he was not one of the shadow-things.

"Luther, I see the way out. I've got Janice. Hold onto me."

"Monty?"

"It's Howard. Follow me"

He felt his way around an overturned chair and pulled the other two toward the vertical red line in the corner of the room. The angled lines on the walls were like signposts, pointing at it. He wondered why none of the other coven members were moving toward it? He could hear their screams all around him, yet he felt an uncanny inner calm.

As they drew near the red line, he suddenly knew what they must do.

"Janice, hold onto my hand. Luther, hold Janice by the hand. I'll guide you."

He put his free hand up to the red line and felt it. There was a kind of vibration against his palm. He had to become thin. They all had to get thin. He turned his hand edge-on and carefully slid his fingers into the glowing crack. It widened slightly. Concentrating, he forced his arm in and turned his body sideways. Something seemed to pull his hand and arm from the other side. This made it easier.

"Turn sideways and hold on tight," he said behind him to the others as his shoulder slid into the widening crack of light.

"What's happening?" Janice said.

"Hold on!"

The pull from the other side became irresistible, and all three were drawn through the red crack.

W hat is this place?" Janice asked.

"Some kind of corridor," Luther said.

Lovecraft could hear their words, but when he tried to look behind, he saw only a pearly iridescence that shifted from one pale color to another. He realized that he could not even see his own body, if he still had a body. Monty's body, he corrected himself. Even so, the pull upon his extended arm did not cease, but steadily drew him forward along this corridor of light.

"Are we safe?" Janice asked.

"I think so," Luther told her. "From the shadow-walkers, at least. Howard, how did you find this place?"

"I don't know," he said. "I saw lines on the walls, and they seemed to point to a doorway of some kind."

"A dimensional portal," Luther told him. "You wrote about them in your stories."

"Nothing in my stories was real," he said, anger building inside him. Why couldn't they understand this point? "It was all fiction, based on my dreams."

"Maybe Monty guided him," Janice suggested.

That was a disquieting thought. Was he being controlled by the soul that had vacated his new body?

An irregular patch of darkness formed against the shimmering pastel background and seemed to grow larger as they approached. It was not black but a kind of midnight-blue. When he was nearer he realized that it was shot with thousands upon thousands of stars.

He found himself lying on dew-covered grass beside a jutting stone. There was no transition. One instant he floated bodiless down the luminescent corridor, and the next he lay sprawled on the wet grass. He sat up and looked around.

Janice and Luther lay beside him. They stirred and groaned. At least they were both alive, he thought. The moon in the starry heavens showed that they lay within the angle of two rows of crude standing stones. He heard the lap of water and pushed himself to his feet, using the stone beside him for support. Luther helped Janice up and they stood staring around in bewilderment. For a while none of them spoke.

They were on a small island in the midst of a substantial river. The banks were no great distance to either side, but the swiftness of the current made swimming to them a dangerous prospect. Lovecraft was not a swimmer. He hated the ocean, and as a boy had been too much of a loner to learn to swim in the ponds near Providence. Wherever they were, it was not Providence. Yet there was something about it oddly familiar, like a place seen in childhood and dimly remembered.

He walked out of the angle of stones, which was of no great extent. It had a larger recumbent stone in its midst that was disquieting. It resembled a pagan altar, and made him uncomfortable when he looked at it, so he turned his gaze downstream. The island was on the edge of a city. Not far downstream a stone bridge crossed the water. There were numerous buildings on both sides of the bridge.

Something moved under the bridge. A lantern flickered alight there, and by its glow Lovecraft saw a man lean over a boat that floated alongside a boat landing.

"There's someone under the bridge," he told his companions.

They began to shout and wave their arms in the air. The night breeze at their backs carried their voices to the ears of the man, who saw them and waved back. For a while he stood and did nothing. Finally, he climbed into his boat and started the outboard motor. He reached the island in a matter of a few minutes. They clambered gratefully over the gunnel and settled themselves on the thwarts.

The boatman was on the snowy side of fifty and smelled strongly of rum. His white hair hung over his ears in a disordered thatch, and at least a three-day growth of beard stubbled his chin and cheeks. He squinted at them by the light of the boat lantern, his keen gaze flicking from Lovecraft's paisley shirt to Janice's nose ring and Luther's pony tail.

"On your way to a frat party?"

"Something like that," Janice said with a smile.

"How'd you get on the island?" He used an oar to push his craft away from the weeds and mud back into the current.

"It was a practical joke," Luther said quickly. "Some friends dropped us off and sped away in their speedboat."

The man hawked and spat into the water. He started the engine with its pull cord and sat beside the tiller.

"Damn fool college kids," he said above the motor's roar. "I'll never understand the tricks you get up to."

"Thank you for extracting us from our predicament," Lovecraft said, shaking the boatman's callused hand. "You will be suitably recompensed."

"I don't want your money," the man said. "It's only a Christian duty to get you off the Witch Island after dark. No one in their right mind would strand anyone on that island at night."

"Witch Island? Is that what it's called?"

"It's what some folks call it."

Something about the name he used for the island woke recognition in Lovecraft's mind, but he still could not free the memory that struggled to the surface of his thoughts. He turned and looked behind. In the silvery glow of the moon, he saw a solitary figure standing beside one of the crookedly leaning stones. There was something vaguely sinister in the way the unmoving figure stood and watched them. It was misshapen in outline, as though hunched at the shoulders, but undeniably human.

"You'll have to go back," he said with some urgency. "There's someone still on the island."

"What?" The boatman craned his neck over his shoulder. "Where? I don't see nobody."

When Lovecraft looked again, the figure was gone from its place, and the island appeared deserted.

"Don't worry about it, son," the boatman told him, patting him on the knee. "The moon plays tricks on the eyes. People see all manner of strange things on that cursed island. If I had my way, I'd dynamite it right out of the river."

Lovecraft peered back for several seconds, then settled into his seat. He turned toward the bridge once again. What about it was so damned familiar?

"We're not from around these parts," he said. "I wonder if you would mind telling us where we are?

"Where you are?" the boatman repeated.

The boat slid under the bridge and he guided it with an expert touch on the tiller to the edge of the stone landing.

"Where are we?" Luther asked with more insistence.

"Don't you even know where you are?" The boatman laughed as he tied up the stern to an iron ring. "You damn fools, this is Arkham."

8.

They left the boatman to his work and made their way up from the landing to a dirty street lined with warehouses on its water side, and with a seeming endless number of taverns on its town side. Electric lamps gave adequate illumination for the intoxicated sailors and dockside prostitutes who peopled the sidewalk, which was made not of concrete or stone, but of venerable tar-stained planks. The street surface itself was closely-laid brick.

"This can't be Arkham," Lovecraft repeated for the third time. "I told you both, Arkham is a city of my imagination. It doesn't exist."

"For a materialist, you're reluctant to believe the evidence of your own eyes," Luther said with a trace of wry amusement.

"I'm a man of reason. If my eyes present an image that is fantastic and impossible, I must deny it."

"Oh, for heaven sake, Howard, grow up. We're in Arkham. Deal with it."

In spite of Janice's chiding tone, she followed after Lovecraft, as did Luther.

"Where are we going?" Luther asked.

"We're on River Street, I think," Lovecraft said. "That street ahead should be Garrison Street. I intend to follow it to Miskatonic University, if it exists here."

They walked on in silence up the gentle grade of Garrison Street. Occasionally a street car passed, rolling along on its rails, or an automobile. However, there was more foot traffic on the sidewalk than traffic in the street.

"Is it how you imagined it?" Luther asked.

"Yes, for the most part," Lovecraft said. "But it's oddly different as well. It seems larger and more spread out and more . . . real. Not everything is where I visualized it to be while writing my stories."

"We passed through some sort of dimensional portal," Janice said. "Wherever this is, Arkham is a reality here."

"If Arkham is real, then all the other places you wrote about must also be real," Luther said. "Dunwich, Innsmouth, Kingsport—the whole Miskatonic Valley."

To this Lovecraft made no reply. The possibility was overwhelming in its sinister implications. The world he had created for his stories was scarcely wholesome or safe for its inhabitants. If this truly was witch-haunted Arkham, these streets concealed many terrible secrets.

Miskatonic University campus had the general appearance of a hallowed Ivy League school. Its buildings were of cut grey stone and red brick, its lawns spacious and generously wooded. Due to the late season, they were covered with rustling leaves that moved in the evening breeze. He continued down Garrison Street toward the largest building, which was located in a corner of the quadrangle.

Leading the others into the meandering campus lanes, he approached the fluted pillars of the front entrance with a mingled wonder and apprehension. From the glow of the street lamps he could easily read the words chiselled into stone above the doors—Miskatonic University Library. Students came and went with books cradled in their arms. The library was still open, as he had hoped.

The others seemed willing to follow his lead for the moment. They trailed after him into the warmth of the library and up to the front desk. The young woman behind the desk smiled pleasantly as he approached.

"How may I assist you?" she asked.

Lovecraft glanced around to be sure that no student or professor was near enough to hear his words.

"I want to see the . . . *Necronomicon*."

The smile lost its charm and faded from her lips.

"I'm sorry, but I'm not familiar with that title."

"It's in the restricted books section."

"I see." She thought for a moment. "I'll have to consult the assistant librarian. Follow me, please."

"Call Professor Henry Armitage. I'm sure he'll give me permission to see the book."

She glanced over her shoulder at the wall clock, which showed twenty past eight.

"Professor Armitage has gone home for the night, but I can let you speak to his assistant, Mr. Phineas Grey."

They waited at a table in a reading room in the restricted section of the library. All around them were locked glass cabinets filled with rare or forbidden texts.

"Is the book here?" Luther whispered to Lovecraft. "If you see it on the shelf, I'll smash the glass and grab it, and we can make a run for it."

"They don't keep the really controversial books on display," Lovecraft told him. "The *Necronomicon*, if it exists, will be hidden away in the back, probably locked in some kind of safe."

"This is what Monty wanted us to do," Janice breathed in excitement. "Find the book. I never thought we'd get so close to it."

They fell silent as the desk clerk returned, walking a pace behind a tall young man with wire-frame eyeglasses who wore a three-piece, pinstriped suit. His brown hair was parted down the middle and held immaculately in place by a liberal application of an aromatic oil that made it gleam in the warm golden glow from the reading lamps.

"This is Mr. Grey, personal assistant to Doctor Armitage," the woman said.

Lovecraft stood up and extended his hand.

"My name is . . ." Lovecraft hesitated, ". . . Montague Willifred."

Grey had a warm and vigorous handshake.

"I've seen you around the campus. You're a resident of Seaton Hall, aren't you?"

"Yes," Luther said quickly when Lovecraft did not respond at once. "We're all students."

Lovecraft introduced his companions. Grey seemed fascinated by the purple streak in Janice's hair, and the ring in her nose.

"Forgive my curiosity, my dear, but are you a foreign student?"

"Definitely. I'm totally not from around here."

"About my request –" Lovecraft began to say.

An expression of regret fell across the assistant librarian's narrow face.

"Quite impossible, Mr. Willifred, quite impossible I assure you. Almost no one sees the particular title you named. It is seldom taken out of the vault."

"If only I could talk to Professor Armitage, I believe I could convince him about the sincerity of my intentions."

"You didn't give me time to finish," Grey said with a mild chiding tone, holding up his hand. "It is quite impossible, under any circumstances, because the book was recently stolen from the library."

"But how is that possible, if the book is kept locked up?" Janice asked.

"How indeed? The police are asking that very same question."

"Did anyone see the thief?" Luther asked.

"No one saw anything. The book is examined only at rare intervals. The last time Professor Armitage opened the vault to make it available to a researcher, it was not there. That is all I can tell you, because that is all anyone knows."

"You mean, it just vanished?" Janice said in disbelief.

"Exactly so. I can't say that I'm sorry about it. The book was evil, and in my opinion the university is better off rid of it."

Lovecraft mulled over this information for a few moments.

"May I ask, who was the scholar that requested to see the book?"

Grey shrugged and sniffed.

"I don't see why not. It isn't privileged information. It was a female graduate student from New York University named Holt—Petra Allison Holt. I remember because the police asked for the same information."

"What did she look like?" Janice asked.

"That I can't tell you. She dealt directly with Professor Armitage. I never saw the young woman."

None of them spoke until they were outside, on the steps of the library.

"What do we do now?" Luther asked.

"Is there another copy of the book?" Janice asked Lovecraft.

"There may be one copy near Dunwich, but it is imperfect." Lovecraft shuddered. "I would rather not have to go there."

Janice yawned.

"I'm worn out. I need to find a couch to crash on."

"We don't have anywhere to stay," Lovecraft reminded her.

"Wait a minute, yes we do," Luther said. "Which way is Seaton Hall?"

"I've never heard of that residence," Lovecraft admitted.

They asked directions from students, and found their way to a venerable timber frame house of three stories that had been purchased by the university and divided into student rooms. Janice and Luther lingered in the hallway, pretending to read the bulletin board, while Lovecraft approached the front desk. It was occupied by a bored student who sat reading a textbook.

"Pardon me. I seem to have lost the key to my room."

The young man rolled his eyes.

"Again? What is it now, Willifred? Three times since the beginning of term? The university should start charging you for these spares."

He went to the keyboard behind him and took down a brass key that was labelled 211. Sighing as though the weight of the world rested on his shoulders, he slapped the key down on the desk.

"Here's some advice, Willifred. Take it to the hardware store tomorrow and get some duplicates made, before you lose it."

"I will bear your suggestion in mind," Lovecraft said, taking up the key.

He motioned the others to follow as he mounted the stairs. The clerk at the desk had resumed the study of his book and paid no attention when they edged past him.

Lovecraft fitted the key into the door labelled 211 and let them in. It was a large room for a university dormitory. It held a narrow bed, a writing desk under the window, a bureau with an attached mirror, and a freestanding wardrobe. At the foot of the bed rested a travel trunk. They gathered on the braided oval mat that covered the floor and looked around curiously. Lovecraft's gaze came to rest on a framed pencil portrait that hung on the wall. It was his face—his real face.

"Home at last," he murmured.

9.

"Monty is your biggest fan," Luther explained. "He used to quote us whole passages from your stories."

"He had your sonnet cycle, *Fungi from Yuggoth*, memorized, and would recite the whole thing from start to finish when he was drunk," Janice added.

They both laughed at the memory.

"Do either of you have any idea how Monty came to be attending Miskatonic University?"

They shook their heads.

"He was very deep, very advanced," Luther said, looking around. "He never talked about the ritual work he did outside the coven. That's a rule of magic, Howard. If you talk about what you're trying to accomplish by magic, it won't happen."

"We must search the room," Lovecraft said. "See what you can find concerning Monty's disappearance, or the theft of the *Necronomicon*."

Janice and Luther glanced at each other, but said nothing. Lovecraft realized that he was beginning to take a leadership role. It felt natural to do so, perhaps because he occupied the body of the leader of their coven. In any case, he knew the Miskatonic Valley better than any man alive, having created it for his stories.

"Here's some money," Luther said. "Enough for food and transportation, anyway."

He took a money clip from the upper drawer of the bureau and held it up for the others to see.

Lovecraft continued to dig into the trunk. At the bottom he found a stack of magazines with lurid covers. *Weird Tales*. The editor, Farnsworth Wright, had a positive mania about adorning his magazine with naked or nearly-naked women. Lovecraft took them out and went through them quickly, scanning the title pages. Each was an issue in which something of his had appeared. Montague Willifred had indeed been a fan of his work.

What he found particularly unnerving was that the dates on the magazines continue after nineteen-thirty-seven, the last year he remembered, when he lay in a hospital bed dying of terminal bowel cancer. The stories in them must have been published posthumously. He wondered if one of the issues published the exact date of his death?

"Monty brought this trunk with him from our world," he observed. "These magazines cannot have originated in this reality."

"Hey, guys, look at this," Janice said from the desk.

She spread on its surface several sheets of paper she had removed from one of the drawers.

"It looks as though Monty was making some notes," Luther said, leaning over her shoulder to look at the papers.

On one of the sheets Lovecraft saw a pencil drawing of a wide-mouthed bottle with a small pendant hanging down inside it on the end of a thread. Occult symbols were inscribed around the bottle. Beneath the drawing was scrawled in a hasty hand, "Kingsport—Old Man—House in the Mist."

On the second sheet was the drawing of an ornate, old-fashioned key, and below it two other keys crossed. The words "Innsmouth—Asenath Waite—Ephraim—Washington Street—Devil Reef—Deep Ones hold one key."

The last sheet bore a strange sketch of intersecting circles and angled lines, along with the symbols of the Head and Tail of the Dragon. Lovecraft remembered seeing the same symbols on the wall of Monty's cell at Butler Hospital. Beside this complex pentacle was scrawled "Dunwich—Wizard Whateley—his book defective?—Yog Sothoth *is* the key." The word "is" was underlined three times.

"Three threads to follow, and three of us. It seems almost providential."

"I'll go to talk to Asenath Waite, woman to woman. Maybe she'll open up to one of her own sex," Janice said. "I've always wanted to see Innsmouth."

"Be sure to visit during the daylight hours," Lovecraft cautioned.

"I'll try old Wizard Whateley. Maybe I can get a look at his copy of the book," Luther said.

"Very well. I'll take a bus to Kingsport and see what I can learn there. We'll meet back in this room in three days."

They each took one of the sheets of paper.

"Now I need sleep," Janice said, pulling off her boots. "I'm taking the bed. Either one of you gentlemen is welcome to join me. I don't think the bed will hold the three of us."

"I'll sleep in the chair," Lovecraft said quickly.

"Chicken," she said, and made clucking sounds.

"Don't worry, Howard, her virtue is safe with me," Luther said. "I only like boys."

They took off their outer clothing to be more comfortable and turned off the light. Lovecraft sat in the desk chair wrapped in a blanket, listening to the others breathing. When their breaths deepened into sleep, he got up quietly and went to the window to peer around the edge of the curtain at the shadows on the deserted street. He watched for a long time, but none of them moved.

10.

Kingsport looked very much as Lovecraft had imagined it for his stories—a small New England fishing port, with antique houses climbing the slope of the hillside from the harbour's edge. In the distance to the north loomed the towering cliffs. It was the first thing he saw when the bus rounded the curve and rattled its way into the town. The hour was late afternoon. Fog lay low over the water of the harbour, giving the twilight scene a dreaming quality. In the air above his head seabirds cried harshly when he stepped off the bus, the only passenger. The town smelled strongly of salt and fish.

He gazed toward the mouth of the harbour, where the fog concealed it, and wondered how far this world of his imagination extended. Had he created it, or had he only glimpsed it across the chasm between worlds? If it had an independent existence, how much of what was in his stories was accurate, and how much had he got wrong?

Turning, he cast his eyes skyward, to the towering lip of the cliff where rested a small cottage of simple but ancient design. It had stood there since before the reckoning of living men, and no history told of its building. He knew this, because he had written it in his stories. When the sea mists rose, the cliff thrust above them like the prow of a great stone ship. The lone inhabitant of that cottage was not of this world or the next, but straddled the two. Lovecraft shivered at the thought. Some things were better left undisturbed.

The bus had let him off on Water Street, which wound around the harbour behind the docks and the decaying warehouses and boat works that lined them. He began to walk slowly along the street, looking at the quaint cottages that occupied the high side of the street. This was the most ancient part of the town, and these simple houses, built by fishing captains and merchant traders for their brief sojourns on shore when they were between voyages, were in the colonial style of the late sixteen-hundreds.

The people of the town nodded to him as they passed but otherwise left him to his own devices. Their faces, browned in the sun and wrinkled by the spray from the sea, had the look of the fey about them. They were honest enough faces, but they kept their own counsel behind shrew eyes. The townspeople carried the air of a past age in the way they walked, in their accent when they spoke, and in the rough but colourful clothes they wore in a style of dress that was almost piratical.

He knew the house he sought by the painted standing stones that decorated the small enclosed front lawn—although, in fairness to the English language, that tangle of weeds and wildflowers scarcely merited the name lawn. The tall, browning weeds clung around the pickets of the fence that enclosed them, some of them bursting forth through gaps between the boards with protean exuberance. They hid the lower trunks of the twisted old trees that shut out most of the light from the cottage, presently losing their leaves due to the lateness of the season. They climbed the rough stones that stood in groups like grotesque sentinels in various places, and threatened to overwhelm the narrow gravel walkway that led to the front door.

He unlatched the gate and entered the yard, then refastened it behind him. It would be prudent to be on his best behaviour, given the studies pursued by the occupant of the house. With some nervousness, he approached the low front door and knocked, then listened. There was no stirring from the other side. He knocked again, more loudly.

"What do ye want?"

The challenge came from behind him and made him flinch. He turned and saw that it was an elderly man. His long white hair framed gaunt cheeks and hung down in front of his shoulders to mingle with his white beard. He appeared as tall and thin as a scarecrow in his long navy-blue peacoat, but there was vigour in his movements and in the glare of his pale grey eyes. He worked the gate and approached Lovecraft along the walk.

"Who are ye, and why the devil do ye bother me?"

His accent and manner of speech were from a previous century.

"My name is . . ." Lovecraft hesitated, wondering which name to use ". . . Howard Phillips Lovecraft. I've come from Arkham to consult with you about a matter of some urgency."

The old man grunted and pushed him unceremoniously aside to open his front door. It was unlocked.

"Urgent for ye maybe, but not for me."

Lovecraft unfolded the sheet of paper he had taken from Monty Willifred's desk and held it up.

"It concerns the object drawn here."

The old man stopped and studied the fluttering paper, then looked hard at Lovecraft.

"Ye'd better come in."

Lovecraft followed him into the main room of the little house. It was sparsely furnished with two arm chairs that faced the fireplace and a long table that occupied the middle of the bare floor. A battered sea trunk rested in the corner, and a tall bookcase covered nearly all of one wall. It was filled with ancient, leather-bound volumes.

Down the center of the table in a row were arrayed a variety of antique bottles in different shades and shapes of glass. Lovecraft counted nine of them. They were partially filled with some kind of discoloured liquid. Small pendulums hung over this liquid, suspended inside the bottles by threads from their stoppers. They were similar to what Monty had drawn in Arkham.

"Sit yourself," the old man growled at him. "I need to look in my books."

Silently, Lovecraft did as he was told. The air inside the cottage had a dank smell, as though it never completely dried. The paneling on the walls was ship-lapped, and appeared to have been calked with oakum in the cracks. A brass hurricane lantern dangled from a chain above the long table.

The old man hung up his peacoat on a hook on the wall, then came to sit in the chair opposite Lovecraft with one of his books. For a time he turned the pages and read various passages silently to himself. Lovecraft wondered that he could see the printed words in so dim a light. The windows were small and dirty, and the beams they admitted did not extend past the table.

The old man closed the black book on his knee with a snap and regarded Lovecraft keenly. After a time, he held up the paper with the drawing.

"Do ye know what this is?"

"I believe it is known as a soul-bottle."

"Do ye know its use?"

"Superstitious folk believe that through magic, the soul of a man may be captured inside the bottle and forced to reveal occult matters by the tapping of a pendulum of lead against the side of the glass."

The old man smiled. It was ghastly to look upon, but Lovecraft gave no sign of discomfort.

"Ye don't believe in such things?"

"No."

"You're an educated man of science."

"Yes."

The burst of derisive laughter caught Lovecraft by surprise.

"There's no fool worse than an educated fool."

"You think me a fool?"

"To come with such as this?" He held up the paper. "And to know nothing about its use? Aye, ye are a fool, but at least ye are a fool who asks questions, so maybe there's hope for ye yet."

This display of contempt aroused resentment in Lovecraft. He wondered if he was wasting his time. Maybe it would be better to leave before he was showered with more insults.

The old man seemed to read his thoughts.

"Take no offense for my rough ways," he said with a wave of his weathered hand, from which the tip of the small finger was missing. "I get few visitors here, and forget the social graces that I learned long before ye were born."

"No offense is taken," Lovecraft lied. "What can you tell me about this drawing?"

The old man studied it for a time before answering.

"These symbols above the bottle are intended to be inscribed on the underside of the cork, and on the lead weight that hangs inside. They are wholly evil in their use."

"How do you mean, wholly evil?"

"I mean what I said. No good can ever come of them. They are the blackest magic and do not originate with our race, but come from outside our world. Those who try to use them fall prey to their corruption."

"What use have they?"

"They are made to bind a master of the art and subdue his will by subjecting his soul to ceaseless torments."

"A binding for a wizard?"

"Aye."

"I come seeking information about the soul of the man who drew these symbols."

"He is damned."

Lovecraft took a few moments to digest this remark.

"Do you mean he is in hell?"

"Hell, you say?" The old man snorted. "He wishes he were in hell, but he is not so fortunate."

"Can you help me to locate him?"

"Ye don't know what ye ask of me. To seek the master of these marks is to sail to your doom."

"I'm not afraid," Lovecraft said.

"Ye should be!" the old man roared. He threw the paper at Lovecraft, who caught it. "I want nothing more to do with ye or your mad quest."

Lovecraft folded the paper and put it into his breast pocket, then stood stiffly, trying to control his anger.

"Very well. I will not trouble you further. I thank you for your hospitality."

He took a step toward the door. At that instant, the lead weights in all the bottles on the table began to tinkle frantically.

The old man leapt to his feet with a furious scowl.

"Damn, ye, you've brought them to my house."

"Brought who?" Lovecraft asked in bewilderment, but got no answer.

He glanced at the windows, and realized that it was nearly full dark outside the dusty panes of glass.

The old man ignored him. He rushed to the windows and looked out, then began to curse with the fluidity and variety that only a seaman can achieve. He went to the table and touched the tinkling bottles, speaking various names as he did so.

"Peters, come forth. Long Tom, there's work to be done. Hear me, Mate Ellis, your captain calls you. Black Harry, Jack, Scar-Face, Spanish Joe, all of ye, come forth and fight."

Lovecraft edged to the windows and looked out. For a moment he saw nothing but the gloom. Then the shadows began to shift and slink behind the trees and stones in the yard.

He turned in time to see transparent wraiths emerge from the tops of the bottles on the table. They arose through the wax seals on the corks in the form of a pale mist and as they went up they expanded and took on the features of men. They formed into full-sized figures in archaic clothing who were armed with daggers and cutlasses, and a savage lot they looked. Lovecraft shrank away from them, but they had no interest in him. They passed through the front wall and the closed front door of the cottage as though these did not exist.

"Now we'll see which crew has the stomach for a fight," the old man said.

"What if they lose?" Lovecraft asked.

The old man stared at him with contempt.

"Then we be both worse than dead men."

Something warned Lovecraft to remain away from the windows. Through their darkening glass he could see swirling shapes flash past, those of misty grey entwined with shapes of black. He thought he saw the flash of steel blades but wondered if he only imagined it. There was no sound.

After what seemed an eternity but could not have been longer than five minutes, the misty grey shapes returned, walking through the wall, and dissolved into narrow columns of smoke-like filaments that slid into the tops of the bottles.

Lovecraft found the courage to go to one of the windows and look out, but the darkness prevented him from seeing anything.

"Ye best sleep here tonight," the old man said without warmth in his voice. "Ye will have a hard climb on the morrow."

11.

Using a portion of Monty's cash, Janice was able to rent the use of an Indian Prince for the day. The single-cylinder motorcycle was ideal for her purposes. It took her a few minutes to learn the obsolete positioning of its controls, but once she got the hang of it, the little bike flew over the unpaved road. The jacket she had found in Monty's closet at Seaton Hall kept her warm. It bore the words Miskatonic University across the back.

The day was clear, the air calm apart from the salt-laden coastal breeze that blew from the sea. She arrived in Innsmouth in early afternoon. Despite Monty's frequent urgings, she had never bothered to read Lovecraft's story about the town, and had no expectations to disappoint, but the chance remarks Monty had made about it intrigued her.

The port of Innsmouth was either picturesque or a ruin, depending on how you looked at it. At one time it had been a thriving hub of industry with a rail head, a prosperous fishing industry, and a gold smelter. Decades earlier a kind of creeping malaise had taken a grip on the community, and had never released it. Job opportunities dwindled. The harbour silted up and was never dredged. The gold smelter cut back on its workforce. Many young people departed for greener pastures, leaving only the old and the infirm to populate the decaying streets.

The people of Innsmouth were an inward-looking tribe descended from Yankee traders. Two centuries of intermarriage had given them all a characteristic cast of features that was referred to as the "Innsmouth look." Their faces tended to be broad, their noses flat, their mouths unnaturally wide. Most were afflicted with a skin condition that made them pale and prone to profuse sweating. Their eyes tended to be protuberant and large. This was more noticeable in the older residents, as Janice discovered while she guided her motorcycle over the decrepit bridges that spanned a small river running through the middle of the dilapidated town.

There were few pedestrians, and those she did see avoided her gaze. The women wore black lace veils that concealed their faces, and the men favoured broad-brimmed hats which they pulled low against the sun. She tried to ask directions to the Waite house from several of them but they all ignored her. She saw curtains move in the upper windows of some of the houses, but no faces at the glass.

Cursing under her breath in annoyance, she killed the engine of the Indian in front of the Gilman Hotel and set the bike on its kick-stand, then made her way inside.

The interior of the hotel was scarcely more inviting than its facade. It had a mouldy smell and the carpets badly needed cleaning. The flowered wall paper hung loose in places and was streaked with water stains, attesting to a leaky roof. To her surprise, the front desk was not empty. A slender young man with deplorable posture stood hunched over the register. She approached the desk and waited for him to look up. And waited, and waited.

Her patience finally came to an end.

"Damn it, look at me!"

She slammed her hand flat on the countertop, making the clerk jump and stare with his bulbous, watery eyes.

"How do I get to the house of Asenath Waite?"

"Who?" he muttered, avoiding her dark eyes.

"Asenath Waite," she repeated with exaggerated slowness. "The daughter of the late Ephraim Waite."

"You have business with the Waites?" he asked suspiciously.

"Yes."

With great reluctance, he gave her directions to the house. She emerged from the hotel and started to straddle the Indian, when she noticed a kind of slime on the seat and the handlebars.

"Great, just great," she muttered.

She looked around and spotted a sheet of newspaper in the gutter. Wadding it up, she managed to use it to clean off most of the clinging, viscose material. She looked around at the windows of the nearby buildings, but no one seemed to be watching her. The street was deserted. Even in the middle of the day, Innsmouth was almost a ghost town.

The Waite house was located on Washington Street in what might be called the wealthy section of the town. Even so, it had seen better days and better decades. It was a large structure with the gambrel roof so common to old timber-frame buildings in New England. The overgrown yard was surrounded by a fence of rust-stained wrought iron. The gate squealed in protest when she forced it open. Dark evergreens screened the house. Passing under them, she mounted the veranda that ran the length of the front and worked the heavy brass knocker on the door.

Much to her surprise, the door opened before the echoes of her knocks faded from the interior. She stood facing a young woman of no great height but with an imposing bearing whose slender body was draped in a long dress of black silk and lace that enclosed her slender neck and arms, and concealed her shoes. Blue-green eyes, the color of the fathomless ocean, lent interest to her otherwise unremarkable features. They protruded somewhat from beneath her drooping eyelids in a way similar to those of the clerk at the Gilman Hotel. Midnight black hair was piled up on top of her head with an elaborate bracing of tortoise shell combs, perhaps to give the illusion of greater stature.

The women regarded each other for several moments.

"I'd like to speak with Asenath Waite."

"I am she. Won't you come in?"

"Don't you want to know why I'm here?"

Asenath smiled, but here eyes did not change.

"I already know why you're here. You want to talk to me about Monty Willifred, who has disappeared from his room in Seaton Hall."

Janice blinked at her in surprise.

"How could you possibly know that?"

She shrugged.

"A likely guess. I know about Monty's occult interests. He and I spoke at length several times at Miskatonic University. I'm a student there myself, you know."

"No, I didn't know."

Asenath stepped aside and gestures for Janice to enter the house.

"We'll talk in the parlour. I was just about to take tea."

They made their way from the entrance hall to a sitting room on the left. It was well furnished but dark—the trees outside blocked much of the light from the windows. They also gave the room some degree of privacy from passers-by on the street, Janice realized.

Indicating for her visitor to sit on the settee, Asenath took a place beside her so that their knees nearly touched.

"What do you study at the university?"

"Medieval metaphysics." Asenath laughed. "An obscure subject, I know, but I find that I have a natural affinity for such things."

"Perhaps you inherited it from your late father. I understand he was a scholar of the arcane sciences."

"How nicely you put it," Asenath said, her eyes sparkling with amusement. "Others have called Ephraim a black magician and things even less polite."

Janice looked around. An ancient French clock on the mantle made a loud ticking. Other than that, the stillness was as deep as that of an Egyptian tomb. She moved her leg away from the other woman's knee, trying not to make it seem like a shrinking gesture.

"His studies must have had a profound influence on you."

"Indeed. Sometimes it seems as though he is here with me still."

A maid entered with a silver tray bearing a china teapot and two china cups. She bowed once and set it on a low table in front of the settee, then withdrew without a word. Asenath poured. She did not ask Janice if she wished milk or sugar, nor were either present on the tray. Janice sipped the tea experimentally. Earl Grey. It was strong and hot.

"The reason for my visit is to ask you if you can help us to locate a certain book. The only copy in the university library seems to have been stolen."

"Ah, yes, the *Necronomicon*."

"You are familiar with it?"

Asenath sipped her tea and set the cup back upon its saucer.

"Not directly. Monty wanted to know if I had read it. I told him that Doctor Armitage had denied me that privilege."

"Why was that?"

She shrugged.

"Who knows? There are certain texts the university guards with great jealousy, and the *Necronomicon* of the mad Arab, Abdul Alhazred, is chief among them. They say that the mere act of reading it drives people insane."

"Yet they permitted access to a graduate student from NYU," Janice murmured. "Strange."

"Maybe she was not who she seemed to be."

"Many people are not what they seem," Janice said, eying her companion, who had managed to scrumptiously move her knee closer so that it now pressed against her leg.

"How true, how very true."

"Is there anything else you can tell me about Monty's occult studies, or his reason for contacting you?"

Asenath cast her gaze up at the painted tin panels that covered the ceiling, giving it the illusion of sculpted plaster.

"Let me see. He wanted to know about the dreamlands, and how he could gain access to them."

"The dreamlands?"

"There's a theory among occultists that it is possible to gain access to the world of dreams while still in the material body."

"What did you tell him?"

"I said that my father had mentioned the dreamlands on a few occasions, although it was never his primary area of study. He told me that the gate of dreams is locked, but that there are three keys by which it may be opened."

"Keys? Do you mean actual physical keys?"

Shaking her head with a smile, Asenath laid her hand gently on Janice's knee. Her fingers felt cold, even through the black leather of the pants.

"No, of course not. What good would a physical key be in the land of dreams? The keys are certain number sequences that have the appearance of magic squares. When the three are placed together in the right order, their numbers cause the dimensions to shift and a passage to open into the dreamlands."

She removed her hand and stood abruptly.

"That reminds me. I promised that I would give Monty the first key. It was in one of my father's books."

Janice rose from the settee. This was more than she had dared to hope. She watched as the other woman opened the drawer of a small writing desk and took out a square of what appeared to be parchment some four inches in size. She accepted it, and saw that a square of three rows and three columns was drawn on it in ink that had faded to a brown color with age. Within the cells of the square were rows of single digit and two digit numbers.

1	5	18
17	21	4
6	16	20

"Do you think this will be helpful?" Asenath asked, stepping close to the other woman, who had to resist the urge to edge backwards.

"I'm sure it will."

"I'm glad. Monty is an interesting young man. A trifle immature and impetuous, but those are common faults of youth that he will outgrow, if he lives long enough."

It was strange to hear this woman, who looked younger than Monty, refer to him as though he were a child.

"I guess I'd better be going. I can't thank you enough for your help."

Asenath put her hand on Janice's shoulder.

"Are you planning to stay in Innsmouth overnight? I really would advise against taking a room in the Gilman Hotel. The service is dreadful. You're welcome to sleep here, if you wish."

"That's really very kind of you, but I'm going to ride directly back to Arkham."

The other woman let her cold hand slide from her shoulder.

"A pity. Just when we were getting to know each other. Perhaps some other time."

12.

"I swear, Monty, if we ever find a way to get you back into your body, I'm going to beat the living crap out of you for putting me through this."

This was muttered under his breath by Luther Cargrave as he pumped the pedals of the decrepit Schwinn bicycle up yet another hill on the unpaved road to Dunwich. The deep ruts and numerous potholes, some filled with dirty water from recent rains, were a cyclist's nightmare. Unfortunately for him, no other transportation had offered itself at the closest train station to Dunwich, a community too small to merit a rail line of its own.

The countryside was dismal. Dark, forested hills seemed to press on either side of the road, their cloaked interiors ominous with silent menace. He knew the shadow-walkers could not move around in bright sunlight, but he suspected they would be able to manifest under the trees of the old-growth forest, where so little sunlight reached the moss-covered ground.

Here and there the trees gave way to small farms, many abandoned but some still worked by stubborn families that knew no other way of life. The uncurtained windows of the farmhouses, with their swaybacked roofs and weathered clapboards, seemed to stare as he passed like blind eyes.

Everywhere he felt a sense of brooding malice. It was not an active hostility but a dull, stupid hatred of all things straight and strong. He shook his head and gritted his teeth as he brought the bicycle over another crest in the road. Sometimes it was more of a burden than a blessing to be gifted with a psychic sixth sense. He had never asked for it, but it was a part of him, and he had learned not to ignore it. Right now it was telling him to turn around and get the hell out of there.

"I can't," he muttered to himself. "I have to see this through for Monty's sake."

The hills became higher and turned into low rounded mountains. They appeared black in the distance, except when their summits were bare of trees. On a few of these bald mountains he saw circles of standing stones silhouetted against the sky like broken teeth. The road continued to become narrower as it pressed between low rock walls formed by piling flat stones one on top of the other. The walls bespoke of a human industriousness in the region's past that was not evident today. They had to be at least a century old. Moss and grass covered their tops where frost heaving had not tumbled the stones into untidy heaps.

He came upon a sagging covered bridge that crossed the narrow stream of the Miskatonic River. Dunwich was located near the headwaters of the river, in the shadow of a wooded mountain. At best the village could not see the sun for more than a few hours a day. There seemed no reason to place a human habitation in such an unfavourable location, yet there it was.

He pedaled through the bridge with trepidation, but the thick timbers were not quite ready to collapse under his scant weight. Dunwich was the shithole he expected it to be. A scattering of moss-covered houses as old as the hills crowded too closely by twisted, ancient trees, almost leafless now due to the lateness of the season. He saw a post office that was closed, a general store in a decaying church with a collapsed steeple, a few other buildings some of which were boarded up. Several of the houses had old rusting car frames and discarded washing machines as lawn ornaments, not that any lawns could be seen amid the tangle of weeds and piles of garbage.

An obscenely fat woman was hanging dirty laundry on a clothesline beside one of the shacks. The sheets were covered with sooty patches. Luther stopped the bicycle and stared at them, wondering how the soot came to be there, and why laundry hung up as clean was filthier than any unwashed laundry he had ever seen. The woman became aware of his attention and scowled at him with a mouthful of clothespins.

"Excuse me, but could you tell me how to get to the old Whateley place?"

She didn't answer. She didn't even blink. He stared at her for a dozen seconds, then got back on his bike and pedaled to the general store in the church.

It was the cliché of every country store he had ever read about, only dirtier and more dismal. Three old men sat on wooden chairs around a pot-bellied stove in the middle of the floor. They stopped talking when he entered. By their overalls and flannel shirts they looked like farmers.

"Could one of you gentlemen direct me to the old Whateley farm?"

One of the old men hocked and spat on the floor.

"This is a store, right?"

Silence.

"I'd like to buy something to drink. I'm thirsty. I came a long way on the road."

One of the men unfolded himself and got up from his chair. He shuffled around behind the counter and scratched the beard stubble on his chin, where there was an ugly red patch.

"What do you want?"

"A bottle of spring water would be good."

"A bottle of what? Water, did you say?"

The two men by the stove laughed.

"He said water. He wants to buy water."

"Skip it. I'll have a Coke, I guess."

He reached behind and took a small bottle of Coca Cola out of a glass cabinet. It was room temperature, and covered with dust. Naturally.

"That'll be a nickel."

Luther paid for his drink and started to twist off the cap, remembered that didn't work back in nineteen-thirty something, and opened it with the opener on his Swiss Army knife. The three old-timers watched him with silent intensity. He felt as though he were on stage, entertaining them. He drank from the bottle. In addition to being warm, it was half-flat. Perfect.

"About old man Whateley's place," he said.

"You'd be smart to stay away from there, young feller," one of the men by the stove said.

"Let's say I'm a dumb fucker. Where would I go?"

"Is that a pony tail you got there?" the man who had spat on the floor asked with a crooked grin. "Ain't that a little girlie?"

"I just want to look pretty, is all."

The men laughed in derision. Luther felt the control on his temper slipping, but fought to hold on. It would accomplish nothing to blow up at these idiots. From his point of view, they didn't even really exist. They were figments of Lovecraft's fictional Miskatonic Valley. He had to admit, though, for fictional characters they smelled real enough.

"One more time—how do I get to the old Whateley place?"

The store owner finally took pity on him, of maybe just got sick of looking at him, and gave him directions.

"Thanks," he said, and set the half-finished Coke down on the counter. He turned to leave the store.

"No one goes out to see Wizard Whateley who knows what's good for him," one of the seated men said to his back.

Once on the bicycle and riding under the trees along the narrow road, he realized the old farts had tried to warn him.

The Whateley farm was completely surrounded by forest, hidden from the road except by a narrow lane that was almost closed by the drooping tree branches crowding together from either side. The house and barn were both large structures badly in need of repair. Boards covered the windows on the second floor of the house. Probably the glass was broken out and old Whateley had no money to fix it. A rusting Packard truck was parked in front of the house, one of its rear wheels off and the hub supported on blocks of wood. He dismounted and rested the bicycle against the side of the truck.

As he approached the front porch, an old man with a long grey beard stepped out the door and stood with his hand on one of the square wooden posts that supported the porch roof. A length of knotted rope held up his worn work pants in place of a belt, and his undershirt was stained with tobacco juice and had several large holes.

Through the screen door behind him, Luther saw a woman's face, her pinched features twisted in an habitual expression of hostile suspicion. She looked neither young nor old, and he found it impossible to judge her age.

"That's far enough," the man said, voice cracked with age but still carrying the bite of authority.

"I'm looking for Wizard Whateley."

"What do you want him for?"

"I need his help."

"What kind of help?"

"Magic."

Whateley straightened and dropped his arm to his side.

"Have you brought money to pay for it?"

"I've got money."

The old man spat off the porch.

"You'd best come inside, then."

There was a smell inside the house that Luther could not identify, but it was infinitely disgusting.

The woman shrank back as they entered the parlour. Luther realized that she was simple-minded. In her arms she carried a bundle. A small pink hand escaped the blanket and waved in the air.

"That's Wilbur, my grandson," the elder Whateley said with pride when he noticed where Luther's gaze rested. "He'll do great things by and by."

Something about the way the lower half of the bundle squirmed in the woman's arms made Luther shudder inwardly, but he took care not to show it.

Whateley went to the rustic stone fireplace and took down from its broad mantle an ancient book bound in crumbling black leather. The cover showed signs of crude repair. He set the book on the seat of a wooden chair and lifted the cover to take from under it a single sheet of paper. This he passed to Luther, who saw that it bore a square grid, the cells of which were filled with seemingly random numbers.

8	12	22
10	23	9
6	16	20

"What's this?"

"What you come looking for. I drew it up last night."

"But how did you know what I needed?"

Whateley chuckled.

"Let's just say a little bird told me."

Luther studied the paper, turning it over. Nothing was written on its back.

"What am I supposed to do with this?"

"That there's the first key, you fool. You won't get through the gate without the three keys."

He remembered the paper in Monty's dorm room with the three keys drawn on it.

"How much?"

"Hundred dollars."

"That's a lot of money. I didn't bring that much."

"Fifty dollars."

He took out his wallet and extracted two twenties and a ten. That left him just about enough for train fare back to Arkham and something to eat while waiting for the train at the station. He folded the key and tucked it away in his wallet. Maybe Janice would know what to do with it, or Lovecraft. He didn't have a clue. His eyes strayed to the book on the chair.

"Is that what I think it is?"

Whateley's red-rimmed eyes narrowed.

"It might be."

"May I look at it?"

"It'll cost you."

"I haven't got much money."

"What have you got?"

"I can spare maybe ten dollars, but that's it."

"Give it here."

The old man stood over him and the squint-eyed woman watched from the corner of the room with the squirming bundle still cradled in her arms as he opened the heavy cover and began to leaf through the pages. His heart fell. The book was in wretched condition. The initial leaves were missing entirely—it was impossible to judge how many—and some of the rest were torn or missing corners, in addition to having been gnawed at the edges by rats and riddled with worm holes.

The book seemed to fall open naturally to a place near the middle, where he read a passage in Latin, mentally translating it into English as he went:

"He is ever the trickster, ever the player of fools, and his malice knows no bounds, for he hates the purity of human souls, which, be they never so stained with black, are yet shining in comparison to his own murked essence. Through the world he walks in many guises, and one mask gives place to another, and yet others, so that no man has seen his true visage. The mighty warrior-priest Cthulhu fears to challenge him, and the opener of ways, Yog-Sothoth, heeds his will, though unwillingly, for he is the hand and eye and tongue of Azathoth. With jealous care he guards the higher mysteries. Many a scholar who thought to open the portal of death has met him while walking alone on the sands, and none has ever returned."

Whateley snapped the book shut.

"That's enough."

Luther straightened his back. He had no money to buy another look inside the book, even were the old man predisposed to grant permission, and everything about the set of his shoulders said that he would not.

"If I brought more money, would you sell me the book?"

"No."

"Not even if I brought a lot more money?"

"This will always be the Whateley book. I got it from my grandfather, and my grandson, Wilbur, will get it after I am dead."

A loud thud from above their heads shook the whole house. Luther looked up at the ceiling in time to be showered with dust. He blinked it out of his eyes.

"What was that?"

Wizard Whateley smiled wickedly.

"I expect that was Wilbur's twin brother. He's big for his age."

Luther heard the timbers above groan, as through from the shifting of some enormous weight. He left the house without another word and rode the bicycle out of the farmyard as though pursued by devils, a crawling between his shoulder blades telling him that something watched without eyes through the boards that covered the upper windows.

THE LOVECRAFT COVEN

13.

It took Lovecraft longer to reach the summit of the northern cliff than he expected. He knew more or less which way to go to ascend the forested western slope from the description in one of his stories, and when he passed Hooper's Pond he was sure he was on the right path, but there were details in the landscape that he had not imagined for his fiction. Once he left the back roads and entered among the trees, the ground cover was dense, and there were many deadfalls to climb over or work around.

He had left the house of the old man in early morning, confident that he could attain his goal by noon, but it was afternoon before he began to gain any significant elevation. He found himself sweating and leg weary, and began to wonder if he would reach the little house on the cliff edge before nightfall. The days were short at the end of October.

It was some consolation that the night-walkers were confined to darkness or shadow. The fall of the leaves had opened the woods to sunlight. He avoided the denser stands of trees where the shadows lay thickest, and was reassured when he peered into them and saw no furtive movement.

A kind of cool mist fell across the forest. For a time Lovecraft assumed it was fog. Then he realized that he had climbed into a low-lying cloud. The sun shining down upon it made it glow with a kind of luminous gold. If he was among the clouds, he thought, he must be close to the top.

He heard a growl from somewhere behind him, and when he turned he caught the flicker of a black shape running behind the trunks of the trees. It was not a shadow-walker, but something low to the ground that moved on four legs. He heard its paws rustle across fallen leaves. A dog, most likely. Were there feral dogs in the woods outside Kingsport? He had never written any into his stories, but it was not unlikely that they should exist.

A lone dog represented little threat, but when a second appeared, and a third, he knew that they were stalking him. They moved in a crescent behind him, cutting off his retreat down the slope. He had no choice but to continue upward. In spite of his shaking legs, he quickened his pace. The growls behind him came more often, accompanied by the snap of teeth. It was strange the dogs did not bark. Surely a pack of feral dogs would bark. The way they slunk through the trees and kept the same distance seemed unnatural. It was as though some higher intelligence guided them.

He snatched up a fallen branch and swung it against the grass to test its strength. It would serve for a makeshift bludgeon, if the dogs attacked. At any rate it was better than no weapon at all. Dogs did not frighten him. While a young boy he had played with mastiffs, and this early experience had forever removed any fear of lesser dogs. Even so, he had no illusions about his chances, should all three of the beasts attack at the same time. They were large and had a wolfish appearance, to judge by the fleeting glimpses he caught of them when he glanced over his shoulder.

The trees opened onto a great chasm that ran across the ground, and he realized that he had reached the top. The depression had been formed by the edge of the cliff starting to break away from the main mass of rock, creating a fissure that was too wide to leap across, and some ten feet deep from its edges to its rubble-filled bottom. At some moment in the future, the great mass of rock on the seaward side of this fissure would sheer off and fall majestically into the sea, carrying the little house with it, but there was no way to predict when that day would come.

Through the trees on the other side of the depression he saw the house. It was a tiny one-room cabin that was sheathed in ancient clapboards that were a silver-grey from centuries of weathering. Cedar shakes of a similar color served to shingle its steep-pitched roof. No door was visible on its westward facing side, but there was an ancient casement window with numerous small panes of bull's-eye glass. The chimney leaned slightly and was ragged at the top where several bricks had fallen out.

All this Lovecraft gathered during the instant it took him to throw his body into the fissure and slide down its steep side. He ran across the weed-choked bottom and clambered up the other side, using the trunks of small trees that grew from its cracks to aid his climb. When he reached the top, he looked back across the divide. The dogs had halted at the edge and appeared confused. They ran from side to side, growling and slavering, their white canine teeth exposed.

For a few moments he dared to hope that the fissure would prevent them from attacking him. Then the leader of the pack, a large black German shepherd with enormous wolf-like ears, edged over the lip and slid down into the fissure. The other two dogs began to follow. Lovecraft did not wait to see if they found a way up the other side. He had no doubt that they would do so. He hurried toward the house.

The only door, he knew well enough, was unreachable. It faced the east, and the foundation of the house rested on the very lip of the cliff. There was no possibility of edging along it to reach the door. He hurried to the casement window and found it latched shut, but did not give up hope. The house had other windows, one in the northern wall and one in the southern wall. He made his way to the north side.

"Let me in," he yelled as he ran. "I'm being chased by mad dogs."

The northern window was also latched. Cursing in frustration, he returned the way he had come and tried the south-facing window. Latched. He heard the dogs scrabbling up the side of the ravine. In desperation he used his stick on the casement. The old window might look ready to fall apart under its own weight, but its leading was tougher than it seemed. The blows of the heavy branch made no impression on it. Throwing it down, Lovecraft searched over the grass for a rock, but saw nothing the right size that he could get out of its socket in the earth in time to do him any good.

Through the thin line of trees along the fissure he saw that the first dog had managed to drag itself out of the depression. It stood staring at him with murderous eyes, waiting for its companions to join it. When they were together, Lovecraft had no doubt they would attack, and then his best course would be to throw himself off the edge of the cliff. As frightening a prospect as it presented, it was better than being eaten alive.

He noticed that a young pine tree grew close to the corner of the house. It was bent and twisted by the constant sea winds that beat against the cliff. One of its boughs hung over part of the roof.

Casting aside the stick, he started to climb. He was about six feet above the ground when the dogs attacked. They were as silent as they had been while hunting him. He felt jaws close around the heel of his shoe and managed to shake them off. Peering down, he saw that all three beasts were leaping into the air to snap at his feet. He pulled his legs up and managed to get above their jaws. Their eyes were not the eyes of normal dogs. They glared up at him with pale hatred, and there was intelligence mingled with their inexplicable malice.

He could wait in the tree in the hope that the old man, who was the sole tenant of the house, came home and opened a window to admit him, but he had no way of knowing if the old man was even still alive, and how would he make his way from the tree to the window without getting killed by the dogs? He could simply stay where he was and wait until the dogs grew bored and wandered off, then descend the western side of the cliff and make his way back to Kingsport. He looked down at the black dog that was the leader of the pack, and saw no reason to expect that it would lose interest. Its grey eyes remained fixed on him with murderous intensity.

The final option did not appeal to Lovecraft but he saw no way to avoid it. With a resigned mind but a fluttering heart, he lowered himself from the bough of the pine onto the steep roof of the house. The grey shingles on the roof were more than an inch thick and their rough surfaces offered a good grip for his body. He edged himself slowly up toward the peak by sliding his hip and thigh along the roof, the palms of his hands flat on the shingles for a better grip.

It was only when he climbed over the peak and began to lower himself along the eastern side of the roof that the folly of what he was doing struck him with full force. He looked over the edge of the roof. The clouds below formed a kind of golden carpet. Through a gap between them he saw the tiny houses and streets and church spires of Kingsport. This must be what it's like to look down on the ground from inside a dirigible, he thought. He wondered how long he would fall, should he tumble off the roof.

What he proposed to attempt was almost impossible. The eve of the roof projected no less than two feet beyond the front wall of the house. Even if the door were unlocked, how could he possibly open it while hanging from the edge of these weathered, rotting grey roof shingles?

As he slid ever nearer to the edge of the steeply-pitched roof, the world seemed to open before him on a golden void of limitless extent. He could feel the vastness of empty air in his toes. It pricked at them like little needles. His heart thundered in his chest. The shingles were loosening. He could not have crawled back up over their sliding backs even had he wished.

With his head near the edge and his eyes closed, he reached one arm around the eve and felt its underside. To his enormous relief he felt a rail of wood that offered a grip for his hands. He had feared he would find it smooth, and then the only course would have been to fling himself into empty space. In Roman times it was a common belief that those who fell from a great height died before they struck the ground. Lovecraft fervently hoped it was true.

How was he to grip the rail on the underside of the eve firmly enough to avoid falling when he allowed his body to slip off the roof? The angle for his hands was wrong. He began to slide down the shingles and turned himself until his body stretched full length along the very edge of the roof. He extended one leg back up the slope, and slowly, with exquisite care, pulled his shoulder beyond the edge so that he could turn his upper body back toward the house.

The front door was located in the middle of the wall, he knew. He must be directly above it. He managed to reach one hand under the eve and grip the wooden rail. The other hand was not in a good position. He could not reach the rail with the other hand until he extended himself still further beyond the roof. He edged forward until his entire torso hung above the clouds, and just as his legs started to slip down the shingles he managed to grasp the rail with the fingers of his other hand.

His body fell off the roof, and he hung from his two hands, unsupported in any other way. Slowly, he straightened his arms and looked under the edge of the eve. He saw the weathered planks of the door, but they were so far away! There was nothing to stand on. The rock foundation of the house was flush with the edge of the cliff. The casement windows on either side of the door were tightly closed, their translucent bull's-eye panes of glass offering no glimpse of the interior.

He lifted one leg and extended his foot to press against the door. It did not open, nor had he expected it to do so. Even if it had been gaping wide, he could not have swung himself through it without falling. He was no acrobat. Already his hands were at the limit of their strength. He could hold on for only a few seconds more.

He looked up at the underside of the eve for handholds by which he could work himself closer to the door, but there were none. In desperation, he swung back and kicked the door with both feet. He did this three times, but the door remained firmly shut. Then he lost his grip and fell.

14.

Howard Lovecraft blinked the sleep from his eyes and looked around. For a few moments he did not know where he was. Then he remembered. He had curled up on one of the wingback leather arm chairs in the library to read, and had fallen asleep. Some-one had wrapped a blanket around him while he slept. Glowing embers in the grate of the fireplace warmed the side of the chair, making the leather hot to the touch. He had been reading the *Arabian Nights*. Now where was the book? He slid from the seat of the chair and found it on the rug.

He remembered having such a strange dream. All about being in someone else's body and being chased by shadows, and . . . what else? The details of the dream slipped away even as he tried to remember them.

"So you're awake, Little Sunshine," his mother said.

She put aside her embroidery hoop and smiled at him. Sunlight from the big window touched the side of her face. He realized that she was beautiful.

"I wish you wouldn't call me that," he said. "It's a baby name."

"You're still my little baby."

"No I'm not! I'm a big boy."

"Did you have a good sleep?"

"I had a funny dream."

He tried to tell her about it, but realized that he only remembered a few bits and pieces. It was so frustrating. His mother listened patiently, shaking her head and smiling.

"You are a strange child. Your head is always filled with such notions. I can't imagine where you get them."

His Aunt Annie appeared at the library door.

"Awake again, is he? Howard, your grandfather wishes to speak with you in his study."

"What about?" the boy asked.

"Why don't you go and find out?" his mother suggested with a smile.

He made his way down the long hall of the Phillips mansion. It was the only home he had clear memories about, although if he tried he could dimly recall living in other places when he was scarcely more than an infant. After his father entered Butler Hospital for his ill health, his mother brought him to his grandfather's mansion on Angell Street, where she herself had grown up.

His grandfather sat behind his writing desk, wearing his usual three-piece suit with its pin-striped vest and gold watch chain. He puffed on a cigar and peered through his wireframe eyeglasses at documents that were spread out before him. Lovecraft saw by their length that they were legal papers—his grandfather had once told him with a twinkle in his eye that lawyers used paper that was longer than usual because they always had so many extra words to write down.

When the old man realized the boy was in the doorway, he smiled and motioned him over.

"Come in, my boy, take a seat. I have something to show you. Just let me finish with these contracts first."

Lovecraft waited patiently, kicking his feet in the air beneath his chair and watching the sparrows in the tree outside the window. Finally, the old man exhaled deeply, blowing a cloud of blue smoke across his desk, and gathered up the legal documents, putting them away in a drawer.

"Is something wrong, grandfather?"

"Just business, boy, nothing for you to worry about. You've got many years ahead of you before you need to bother about such things."

"I want to help you with your work when I grow up," the boy said.

"And you will, Howard. I know you will. You're smart as a whip."

He pushed himself up from his chair and stepped around the desk.

"Come with me. I have something to show you."

"What it is?" the boy asked, sliding out of his chair and following.

"Something wonderful. You just wait until you see it."

Bursting with curiosity, he followed his grandfather up the stairs to the second story of the big house, and up the small flight of steps that led to the attic. It was dusty up there, and cobwebs hung from the exposed rafters of the roof. The light that came through the round windows at each end of the house was not enough to dispel the shadows in the corners. For some reason this disquieted the boy.

"Come over here," the old man said.

He knelt down before a dusty travel trunk the boy had never noticed before and unlocked it with a small key on the end of his watch chain. Opening the lid, he motioned the boy closer. Howard peered over his shoulder to see into the dark interior of the trunk. His grandfather felt around in its bottom and drew forth a bundle of black cloth that was tied up with black cord.

"This is your legacy, boy. When I was your age, my father showed it to me, just as I am showing it to you."

"What is it?" the boy asked in wonder.

"This is the Phillips' family treasure, Howard. It is the reason for all our success and happiness. When you become a man, it will be yours. You must never lose it or let it fall into the hands of anyone else. Once it is lost it can never be regained. Do you understand?"

"Yes, grandfather."

With trembling fingers, the old man tugged at the black cord and undid the bows that held the bundle together. Lovecraft realized that it was not the first time he had seen his grandfather's fingers shake. The health of the old man had not been good lately. He had overheard his mother whisper to her brother that there had been setbacks in his business investments.

The black cloth fell open to reveal a large silver key that had gone black with tarnish. The head of the key had three ornate loops, and he saw that it was covered with fine filigree work, inlaid into the silver with thin gold wire. Something was wrapped around its shaft— a scrap of paper. The old man passed the key to him.

It was surprisingly heavy. He examined it, turning it this way and that.

"What's it for, grandfather?"

"This is the key of dreams, Howard. When you are older, you will know what to do with it. Your last name may be Lovecraft, but you are a Phillips by blood."

He uncoiled the paper. It had a stiff, unnatural feel, and he realized that it was not paper at all, but parchment. On it was drawn in black ink a square divided into rows and columns by grid lines. Inside the cells of the square were numbers.

15	25	2
1	14	27
16	3	13

He stared at them without comprehension. Some little voice deep inside told him that they were important, but he could not see how.

Suddenly he felt overwhelmed with fatigue. His head swam and he had to sit down on the floor to avoid falling down. Clutching the key and the parchment close to his chest, he lay back on the floor and closed his eyes. He heard his grandfather's voice, anxious with concern.

"What's wrong, my boy? Do you feel sick?"

"I'm just tired, grandfather. Very sleepy," he heard himself murmur in the darkness.

His grandfather said something else, but Lovecraft did not hear it. He was already asleep.

15.

Awareness returned to Lovecraft with the abruptness of a stretched rubber band that snaps back on itself. He jerked with his entire body and half sat up. A nut-brown face surrounded by wild black hair and a full black beard hung over him, and gentle hands pressed him firmly down by the shoulders. He looked around, bewildered, and realized that he lay on a wooden table. Two wooden chairs stood beside the table. In one corner he saw a brick fireplace of antique design. Three of the walls of the room had a single small window, and in the fourth wall a pair of windows stood on either side of a plain door of stout oaken planks.

"I'm inside the house on the cliff," he murmured.

"Yes, that's right," the little man said, nodding his head.

"I fell from the roof."

"Nodens caught you in his ship of dreams, and I brought you inside my house."

"Nodens is a god."

"Yes, he is." The other man's brown eyes sparkled. "It was lucky you fell when you did. A minute sooner or later, and he would never have caught you. He was bringing me home when you landed on the deck of his ship."

"But gods aren't real," he murmured. "They're just fairy stories."

He drew several slow, deep breaths, then pushed himself to a sitting position on the table. He stood up. The floor seemed to spin away. He grabbed the edge of the table for support.

"Poor man, sit down before you fall down," his host told him with concern.

He allowed the little man to help him sit in one of the chairs. His thoughts were strangely unclear, so that he had to concentrate to remember why he had climbed to the house. Feeling in his pocket, he drew forth a Spanish gold piece.

"This is for you. The old man of Kingsport said you're recognize it."

The gnome-like little man took the gold coin and studied both sides. "You've been to see him, then?"

Lovecraft nodded.

"He told me to come here, that you would answer my questions."

This seemed to surprise the little man.

"Did he, did he, now? Well, well, I must try not to make him a liar."

Lovecraft forced himself to his feet, waving off the concern of his host, and went to the casement in the southern wall. There was no sign of the dogs. He peeked out the western and northern windows in turn, but the dogs had retreated back across the ravine. Returning to his chair, he related all that had happened to him since waking up in the cell at Butler Hospital.

"Did Monty Willifred come here?"

The other shook his hairy head.

"I don't get many visitors. You're the first in, oh, so many years."

"Can you tell me what's happened to me? Why am I inside his body? Shouldn't I be dead?"

The little man went to the fire and stirred the pot that hung near its embers. The rich aroma of rabbit stew filled the air, and Lovecraft realized how long it had been since his last meal.

"You say your friend was searching for the *Necronomicon*?"

"That's what the members of his coven told me. They don't know why he wanted it."

"That book has a powerful guardian who prevents its use by men."

"But many have read it," Lovecraft pointed out.

"Many have read small parts of it, and gone mad or killed themselves. Or they have met with accidents. Why do you suppose that is?"

"In my stories, it is the content of the book that drives them mad."

The other shook his head.

"When the book is read, he knows. He comes to them. If they try to make use of the knowledge in the book, he deals with them."

The little man brought two bowls of stew back to the table and set spoons beside them. They began to eat. Rabbit stew. Lovecraft found it surprisingly good.

"Are you saying that Monty read the *Necronomicon?*"

"Some of it, at least," his host agreed. "That alerted the guardian of the book."

"What happened to him?" Lovecraft asked, forgetting the spoon halfway to his lips.

"He sealed your friend in a soul bottle and carried him into the dreamlands, leaving his body empty."

"But why did I come into his empty body?"

The little man shrugged his shoulders beneath his cascade of black hair.

"You said your friend was obsessed with your stories, and was your direct descendant by blood. Some affinity drew you into his body at the moment of your death."

"How am I to find him and return him to his body?"

His host studied him seriously for several seconds with his brown eyes.

"Are you sure you want to?"

"What do you mean?"

"If his soul returns to his body, yours will be forced out, and you have no receptacle of flesh."

Lovecraft felt a creeping dread as his words hit home.

"What would become of me?"

"That I can't say for certain, but there is a good chance that you would become a revenant."

"You mean, a ghost?"

"A hungry ghost, wandering and lost."

Lovecraft set down his spoon, his appetite suddenly gone. He was coming to the realization that there could be no happy outcome for him. Either he remained trapped in someone else's body in a strange alternative world, or he became a wandering homeless shade.

"The book was stolen from Miskatonic University Library," he said.

"Its guardian stole it, to prevent you and the others from reading it."

"Does this guardian of the book have a name?"

The little man met his eyes.

"I would prefer not to speak it in this house. We are on the boundaries of many worlds here, many realities, and a word spoken here can be overheard by too many ears."

Nothing Lovecraft said would persuade him to reveal the name of the guardian.

16.

When Lovecraft arrived back at Monty's room in Seaton Hall, he found Janice and Luther waiting for him. They had already compared notes. He took the chair at the desk while they sat side by side on the bed, and he related to them all that had passed in Kingsport. Janice told of her surprising encounter with Asenath Waite, and Luther reported the events in the Whateley farmhouse.

"It's as though Monty was being guided," Janice said with excitement. "At each of the three places he left clues about in his notes, a numerical key was waiting."

"Somebody wanted us to find the keys," Luther said. "We've been playing around with the numbers on our squares, but we can't make out any overall pattern."

"Luther's really good with cryptography and puzzles," Janice said.

"If I were really good I'd understand how the key works," he objected ruefully.

Lovecraft took out the paper with the number square he had copied from his dream.

"Maybe this will help. It's what I saw in my dream, wrapped around the silver key in the trunk in the attic. The symbolism of the silver key can't be accidental."

"In your stories, Randolph Carter uses a silver key to access the dreamlands," Luther said.

He took the paper and carried it to the desk, where the other two squares rested. Studying them, he fell silent and began to jot down notes in a notebook. Lovecraft slid his chair further away to give him more room.

"Who's Randolph Carter?" Janice asked Lovecraft.

"Haven't you read my stories?"

"To be honest, not many of them. I don't like reading fiction. It's just not my thing."

"Yet you were with Monty in a coven that bears my name."

"I was *with* Monty," she said, emphasizing the third word. "I would have been with him if he had founded a society to collect antique gumball machines."

"Randolph Carter's an explorer of dreams," Luther murmured, his head bent over the desk. "In the Carter stories, dreams are real and Carter is able to enter them while retaining his full awareness."

"I always thought the silver key in the trunk in Carter's attic was my invention," Lovecraft said. "Now I'm not so sure."

"What do you mean?" Janice asked.

"When I went back to my grandfather's house on Angell Street, it didn't feel like a dream. It felt more like a memory."

"You mean you might have been shown the silver key by your grandfather as a young boy, forgot about it when you got older, and then recreated it in you fiction?"

Lovecraft nodded.

"It's called a recovered memory," Luther murmured. "They're usually not very reliable."

He slammed his palm down on the surface of the desk, making the others flinch.

"Got it!"

"Got what, for Christsake? You scared the shit out of me," Janice said.

Luther's eyes shone with delight. He motioned them over to the desk. They crowded beside him and stared down at the three number squares, which he had laid out in a row.

"My mistake was in trying to combine the cells of the squares by addition, to make a fourth square," he said with a hand on each of their shoulders. "I was thinking two-dimensionally."

"Was that bad?" Janice asked.

"It was fatal. I never would have seen the pattern. I had to think outside the box, as they say."

"What does that mean?" Lovecraft asked.

Luther chuckled and patted him on the shoulder.

"I keep forgetting that you're not from our time. It's an expression that means to think in radical and unconventional ways that transcend normal boundaries. You know, like when Alexander the Great cut the Gordian Knot?"

"I don't get it," Janice said. She shrugged Luther's hand off her shoulder with annoyance and straightened her back.

"There's a folktale that when Alexander the Great visited the city of Gordium, he was challenged to solve the puzzle of the Gordian Knot," Lovecraft explained. "That was a very complex knot that was tied around the shaft of an ox cart. The challenge was to untie it and remove it from the shaft. For centuries no one had ever been able to do it because the knot was so complex."

"The story goes that boy-wonder Alexander didn't even try to untie the knot. He just took out his sword, and with one stroke cut the knot in two, thereby removing it from the shaft and solving the riddle," Luther said.

"In the version I learned, he merely unhooked the shaft from the cart and slid the knot off the end," Lovecraft told her.

"It doesn't matter," Luther said. "What matters is that he thought outside the box. These three squares are two-dimensional, so I was expecting to combine them in some two-dimensional way."

He picked up the three sheets of paper and held them one above the other, separated by several inches.

"It was only when I thought in three dimensions that I realized the answer."

Lovecraft stared at the papers for several seconds.

"It's some kind of three-dimensional geometry."

"It's even better than that," Luther said with delight. "It's a magic cube! An order three magic cube!"

"What's a magic cube?" Janice asked.

Luther looked at Lovecraft, who inclined his head for the young man to continue.

"A magic cube is a three-dimensional magic square."

"You mean like the planetary squares in Agrippa's *Occult Philosophy*?"

"Exactly. A magic square is a square grid of numbers, where the sum of the numbers in each row, each column, and each diagonal is the same. Now, in a magic cube, magic squares are stacked one on top of each other so that these same magic qualities hold true, but in three dimensions."

"How many magic cubes are there for squares of nine cells?" Lovecraft asked.

"Exactly four," Luther told him. "There are a lot more minor variations that can be generated by turning and tilting these four cubes, but there are only four truly unique cubes."

"And these squares make up one of them?"

Luther nodded, eyes shining with delight.

"What gave me the clue is that all three squares combined contain the numbers from one to twenty-seven. There are twenty-seven cells in a magic cube of order three—that is, a cube three cells tall, three cells wide, and three cells deep."

"I think you've found the answer," Lovecraft told him. "Congratulations."

"I'm sure of it," Luther said with conviction. "I didn't see it before because the highest number on Janice's square is twenty-one, and the highest number on my square is twenty-four. When I saw that the highest number on your square is twenty-seven, and that all three squares together contain all the numbers from one to twenty-seven, the solution was obvious."

"But now that we know the key is a magic cube, what do we do with it?" Janice asked.

This silenced the enthusiasm of her companions. The three of them stared down at the papers on the desk. Lovecraft noticed that in addition to the sheets, there were numerous smaller squares of paper, each bearing a single capital letter.

"What are these? A false lead?"

Luther shook his head.

"That has nothing to do with the squares. I was frustrated. When I get frustrated, I like to work on a crossword puzzle or a Sudoku puzzle, but I didn't have any, so I started to think about Petra Allison Holt from NYU."

"Sudoku?" Lovecraft asked.

"A kind of number puzzle. Doesn't matter."

"That's the name of the graduate student who stole the *Necronomicon* from the library here at Miskatonic," Janice said.

"The woman whom we think may have stolen the book," Lovecraft corrected.

"Anyway, I started to play around with the letters in her name, looking for patterns. At first I didn't get anywhere. Then I realized that maybe some of the letters were nulls, and didn't have anything to do except disguise the actual anagram."

"The letters form an anagram?" Lovecraft asked, his interest quickening.

"Brother, do they ever. What I did was take out her middle name, but that didn't work, so I put back in her middle initial. Still no luck, so I started to think that where she said she came from might be important. I put in the letters for New York University, then shortened it to NYU, then realized that the U wasn't needed."

He drew the letters to the middle of the desk and discarded some of them, turning the others upright so that they spelled "P-E-T-R-A-A-H-O-L-T-N-Y. He looked at the others, waiting for their reaction.

"There, do you see it? Do you see it?"

"I don't see anything," Janice told him.

"I'm not sure," Lovecraft murmured. "Wait a moment."

He reached down and began to rearrange the letters of the name. Luther grinned and nodded.

"You got it, Howard."

Janice leaned between them.

"What? What does it spell?"

Lovecraft drew away his hand. The three stared down at the small squares of paper, which bore the letters: N-Y-A-R-L-A-T-H-O-T-E-P.

17.

The shadow-walkers came for them shortly before dawn. They went to sleep in their clothes with the overhead electric light on, Janice and Luther in the bed and Lovecraft curled uncomfortably in the desk chair with a blanket wrapped around his shoulders. At some point, while they slept, the light failed.

Lovecraft awoke to a sense of being smothered in a soft, formless jelly that was neither warm nor cool. Everywhere was blackness. He struggled but could not move his arms more than a few inches. Dimly, as through many layers of ebon felt, he heard terrified cries. The chair saved him. His flailing legs kicked it onto its side, and whatever enveloped his head and torso slipped off. He scrambled away from the dark mass and gained his feet.

By the pale grey light that found its way through the curtains over the window, he saw similar dark shapes on the bed, with the girl and the young man under them, still entangled beneath the blankets. As they thrashed around and sought to free themselves from the pressing weight, these masses of darkness shifted and changed shape. At one moment he saw three separate forms that were almost humanoid, but at the next instant, little more than rippling bags of shadow. The fourth shadow-walker slowly gathered itself into something bipedal and began to creep toward him. It was all the more horrible because it lacked a head.

Janice's terrified face showed itself above the pulsating blackness that pressed on top of her. She stared directly at him.

"Get out of here, you idiot. Save yourself. Get to Monty. Get out of here!"

Lovecraft felt his hand fumble for the doorknob behind him without ever making the conscious decision to flee the room. The door opened just as the blackness pressed up against his chest, and he fell backward through the crack into the corridor of the dormitory, which was dimly lit by a weak wall lamp with an ornate flower-shaped ceramic shade.

The dorm room door snapped shut, as though pushed by some great force, but the screams of the two entangled in the bed still found their way through the panel. Lovecraft could only stand in the hallway and tremble. He was fully dressed apart from his shoes, which he had removed to sleep.

Other doors began to open, and sleepy-eyed students put their heads out, or came into the hall.

"What's happening?" one girl demanded, clutching a housecoat around her neck. Her brown hair was done up in bobby pins.

"It's a fight," a young man in wireframe eyeglasses told her.

"It sounds more like a murder," said another youth. "Somebody, go and phone the police."

The student telephone was on the floor below, at the foot of the stairs. Before anyone could move, an older woman came stalking purposefully along the corridor.

"I've already called them. They're sending a car."

Abruptly, the sounds of struggle stopped. The students looked at each other without speaking. Several of them stared at Lovecraft.

With great reluctance, he forced himself to reach for the doorknob and turn it. The door opened inward. Even in those few minutes, the light from the pre-dawn sky had strengthened enough to show him that the room was empty.

Lovecraft entered warily. None of the students followed. He went to the disordered bed. There was no blood. It was just an empty bed. He bent a knee and lifted the edge of the blankets to peer under the frame, but the space beneath was as empty as the bed itself. He turned slowly, looking around the room.

Never in his life had he felt more alone, or more vulnerable. The shadow-walkers had simply come and taken his companions. They would have taken him as well, but for the luck of his chair falling over. He went to the window and slid wide the curtains with both hands, then stood in that posture, deep in thought, bathed in the chill light of early morning.

When at last he moved, he moved quickly. He put on his shoes, then went to the writing desk and took the remainder of the money from the money clip in the top drawer. Gathering up the three sheets that formed the parts of the key of dreams, he folded them and shoved them into his pocket on top of the money. He had to get out of Seaton Hall before the police arrived. If he answered their questions honestly, they would lock him up in an asylum, and if he refused to answer they would detain him until he spoke. He couldn't risk being trapped in a dark cell overnight. The shadow-walkers would surely come for him, or their master would send something worse.

He slipped out of the room and through the knot of chattering students who hovered in the corridor. The telephone directory was where he remembered seeing it, on a little table beside the student wall phone in the lower hall. He flipped through it with nervous haste. When he found the name he sought, he experienced an almost euphoric sense of relief. Had the name not been in the book, he would scarcely have known what to do next. But the name was there. He committed the address to memory.

As he left the dormitory, the police were just entering. Neither of the uniformed officers so much as gave him a glance.

18.

The streets of Arkham were almost deserted due to the early hour. Only a few grey souls shuffled along the sidewalks, their heads bent and faces emotionless. He walked past them like a ghost unseen to the university library, and sat down on the stone steps beside one of the massive fluted columns, shivering in his thin paisley shirt with his arms folded. The rising red ball of the morning sun cast a slight but perceptible warmth over his limbs that he received with silent gratitude.

An hour or so passed. A few mature individuals entered the library, and some time after them, a larger number of young students. When Lovecraft judged that enough time had passed for the average person to be awake and up from bed, he stood, stretched stiffly, and proceeded across Arkham to the address in the phonebook.

He found it on Sentinel Street near Christchurch Cemetery, in an older but still respectable neighbourhood of the city. The house was large, well kept, but drab. It gave the impression of neglect, even though the porch was swept clear of fallen leaves and the white paint on its clapboards recent. It was unadorned save for thin painted lines of black trim around the windows and front door.

Lovecraft stood admiring the simple, honest colonial architecture of the house for several minutes, then crossed the street and climbed the steps. After a moment of hesitation, he knocked. When no answer came, he tried again, and yet a third time. As he was about to turn away, a shuffle came from the other side of the door, and it opened on a tall man in his late thirties with disordered brown hair. He squinted against the morning sunlight, and Lovecraft saw that he had clear grey eyes.

"Who the devil are you, and what do you mean by banging on my door at this ungodly hour?"

"I'm looking for Randolph Carter."

The other man tightened the silk sash of his quilted, wine-coloured bathrobe around his waist with a gesture of annoyance and stared down at Lovecraft. In his old body, Lovecraft would have been able to meet him eye to eye, but Monty was some two inches shorter.

"I'm Randolph Carter. What do you want?"

"I need to talk with you."

"And your name is?"

"Lovecraft. Howard Phillips Lovecraft."

"Never heard of you. Go away."

Lovecraft prevented him from shutting the door.

"It concerns the dreamlands."

Carter looked at him without speaking for half a dozen heart-beats.

"You'd better come in. Make yourself at home in the library while I get dressed."

Lovecraft found a room on the lower floor that was lined with bookshelves, all of them full of books. An ornately-carved desk occupied the best light with the tall, multi-paned window at its back. On it rested an Underwood Standard typewriter, a sheet of paper still engaged in the roller. Beside it he saw a disorderly stack of typed sheets covered with penciled annotations. As might be expected, no embers remained in the iron grate in the brick fireplace. He shivered as he slid into one of the button-tufted brown leather armchairs. In some ways the room reminded him of his grandfather's study.

It was an indescribably odd sensation to sit inside the house of his own literary creation. He had always thought of Randolph Carter as his better half—the man he himself might have been were he more handsome, braver, and more intelligent. In his stories, Carter faced his fears the way Lovecraft would have wished to face them. He sought out danger to test himself and usually prevailed.

Sounds reached his ears from different parts of the old house. Footsteps. The opening and closing of doors. The slam of drawers and what he took to be the rattle of silverware. Water running from a tap.

Carter returned carrying two steaming mugs. One he set on the corner of his desk, and the other he gave to Lovecraft.

"I hope you like your coffee black."

Lovecraft sipped it with care, and could not avoid making a face.

"A bit strong for you? I boil it in a pot. More flavour that way."

Sitting on the front edge of his desk with one hip, he took up his own cup and drank with obvious enthusiasm. He wore penny loafers, casual tan trousers and a sky-blue pullover sweater. Lovecraft noticed that he had drawn a comb through his hair, although the improvement was minimal.

"Apologies for my lack of manners, Mr. Lovecraft. I was still half-asleep when I opened my door to you."

"Think nothing of it."

"That's a good old English name, Lovecraft. Not very common."

Lovecraft balanced his mug on his knee with one hand.

"Forgive my abruptness, Mr. Carter, but the situation I face is dire, and the lives of others may be at risk."

"Of course, old man, don't mind me. Say what you need to say."

He related to Carter in an unemotional way his awakening at Butler Hospital, his meeting with the members of the coven, the attack of the shadow-walkers on the Willifred house, his flight through the dimensional portal to Arkham, and the acquisition of the three dream keys.

Carter listened with a serious expression, and did not speak until Lovecraft finished.

"That is an extraordinary story, Mr. Lovecraft."

"I know, but it is all true."

"Let me assure myself of several points, if you don't mind. You say you are presently in the body of another man, whose soul has been abducted by shadow monsters."

"Yes."

"When you fled from them, you left your own universe and entered this one, which is entirely the creation of your own imagination."

"Insofar as I have experienced it, yes."

"You are a writer and I am one of your fictional creations."

Lovecraft met his gaze.

"That is correct."

Carter chuckled.

"What a wonderfully fertile imagination. If you created me, then I suppose in a sense you are my God."

"I've never thought of it that way," Lovecraft said, annoyed by his levity.

"Did you create my parents as well? My ancestors?"

"Yes."

"Let me pose a hypothetical question to you—how do you know all this is real, and not just one of your nightmares?"

Lovecraft did not answer at once. It was true that since early childhood he had been prone to the most horrific bad dreams. But how had Carter known this?

"It feels real."

"You've just told me that you created everything. You created me. Nothing in this world is real. Yet here you are, in this world. What does that make you?"

"I know the difference between dreaming and waking. This is real, for me at least."

Carter set his empty coffee mug aside on his desk and studied Lovecraft. The smile was gone from his lips.

"What do you really want from me? Do you hope to work some confidence scheme and separate me from my money? Because, if so, I have to tell you there is little enough to steal."

"I know things about you others cannot know," Lovecraft said quickly. "You fought in the Great War. You were a member of the French Foreign Legion. You knew Harley Warren in Florida, and last spoke to him over a telephone in an ancient graveyard in the Big Cypress Swamp. As a boy you played in the cave known as the Snake Den and were fascinated by it. Your grandfather gave you a silver key —"

"Enough," Carter told him, holding up his hand. "I believe at least that you have studied the history of my life, though where you found out about Warren puzzles me. I told that adventure to no one but the police. If you don't want my money, why have you come to me?"

Lovecraft stood from the chair and set his coffee mug on the desk. He drew from his pocket the three sheets of paper bearing the number squares and showed them to Carter, who studied them with interest.

"These are the parts of the key that will unlock the gate of dreams. I know what the key is, but I need to know how and where to apply it."

Carter nodded, studying the squares. When he returned the sheets to Lovecraft, his expression was sad.

"At one time I might have been able to help you, Mr. Lovecraft, but that time in my life had passed me by. I no longer enter the dreamlands when I sleep, or explore their curious landscapes. The well of my invention has run dry. There is no magic in the books I write these days. I had almost forgotten the dreamlands existed until you mentioned them just now."

"No, you're wrong," Lovecraft told him with passion. "You still have the old gift. You lost it for a time, but it will come back to you stronger than ever. You must trust me in this."

Carter raised a skeptical eyebrow, but it was a good-natured disbelief.

"Because you are my God?"

"If you like. It doesn't matter what you think of me. What matters is that you lend me your expertise in dreaming. Where should I apply this key? How is it to be used?"

With a vague smile, Carter turned and stared out the window for a time. He noticed the sheet of paper in the typewriter, plucked it out with a gesture of annoyance, and crumpled it in his fist before dropping it into a waste basket beside the desk.

"I can't tell you where you are to use the key. For me it was the Snake Den, but for you it may be some other location entirely. I can only tell you that it will be a place of rarest dreams that still hold power in your imagination. There is no use trying to open the gate of dreams in a dead place that has no magic. A place like this old house, for example. It can't be done, I know, I've tried often enough."

"How is the key to be used? Luther said it is a magic cube, and I can follow his reasoning, but that doesn't tell me how I'm to actually apply it."

Carter patted him on the shoulder in a companionable way.

"Think about the nature of dreams. They are not material things, are they? Not from the perspective of our reality, at least. The key to enter them can't be physical, either."

"If it's not physical, what it is?" Lovecraft asked in confusion.

"What are dreams, if they are not physical?"

"States of mind," Lovecraft said. "Dreams are states of mind."

"Wouldn't a key to the dreamlands be a state of mind as well?"

Lovecraft nodded. It made sense.

"But still, how am I to use it?"

"I would suggest that when the proper moment arrives, you hold it in your mind and mentally turn it."

"Can the answer really be so simple?"

Carter shrugged.

"There is nothing complex about dreaming. It requires no machinery. We all do it. The trick is to be aware when you're doing it, and to remember afterwards what you've done."

"You must come with me," Lovecraft said with sudden passion. "You are a much greater dreamer than I can ever hope to become. Together we can solve this mystery and rescue the soul of a foolish young man from his fate."

Carter met his enthusiasm not unkindly.

"You would do that, without knowing what your own fate will be should you succeed?"

"Yes. It's not about just Monty Willifred anymore. It's bigger than that. I feel that I was brought here, into the Miskatonic Valley that I created in my stories, for some higher purpose. I have a role to play in this strange affair that I cannot shirk."

Carter clapped him on the shoulders with both hands.

"Then I wish you well, Lovecraft. It sounds like a rare adventure, but I cannot share it with you. For me, the gate of dreams will remain shut until I find my own key, the one I lost so many years ago."

Lovecraft tried not to show disappointment. He felt so utterly alone, and had hoped that Carter would choose to share the danger. For the first time he realized that this task was his, and could be accomplished only by him, if indeed it was to be accomplished at all.

Carter escorted him to the front door of the house with a companionable arm around his shoulder. He opened the door, then paused to shake Lovecraft's hand.

"I wish you the best of luck, old man. If you ever manage to get back to your own world, write me up some money, will you? It costs a fortune to heat this old place."

"You have some interesting adventures yet in store for you," Lovecraft told him with a cryptic smile.

"Do I? Well, then, I suppose money may not be all that important. Fare you well, Howard Lovecraft. It's not often I meet with a man who is even stranger than myself."

19.

Lovecraft began to walk through the streets of Arkham. He had no destination in mind, so he walked on without seeing where he was going, and as a consequence was almost run over several times. The squawking horns of the cars and trucks made little impression. He had never felt so low in spirit.

Utterly alone, he had no human being to talk to, no one to turn to for help. What he should do, where he should go, were mysteries. He could not return to Seaton Hall, and had very little money left even to buy food, let alone shelter for the night. Not only was he in a strange and hostile city, in an alien universe, pursued by monstrous creatures out of nightmare that tried to kill him, but he did not even know how to get back into his own body, which in any case was probably long dead.

He thought of his short story, "The Outsider," in which a man rises from his own grave, only to discover that his flesh has rotted and that everyone and everything he knew in life have passed away. While writing the story, he could not imagine a more isolated or lonely circumstance, but here he was, outdoing the outsider at his own game.

Someone knocked against his shoulder, half-spinning him around on the sidewalk. He began to shout an angry insult, then held his tongue. The figure was a short but hulking mass of black clothing that hobbled quickly along with the aid of a cane. The shawl-draped head turned, and he saw through a black lace veil that it was an old woman. No, that was too kind a way to describe her. She was an ancient, rotting crone. As if able to read his thoughts, the old woman shot him such a piercing glare of malice that he felt it as a physical blow. Before he could blink twice, she was lost amid the other pedestrians on the crowded sidewalk.

He looked around with awakened awareness, and realized that he had strayed into a run-down section of Arkham. The men and women who hurried past him on the sidewalk were foreign-born labourers, the children loitering in the doorways were ragged and dirty. Even the dogs looked underfed.

It was an ill wind that blew no good, he thought. Rooms for rent were likely to be cheap in this part of the city. He studied the large colonial house before him, and saw that it had been partitioned into a rooming house, like so many others on the street. It had suffered woeful neglect for decades, but sturdy construction and honest materials told their tale. It was still substantially sound, with a solid foundation and a more or less straight ridge on its roof.

There was something eerily familiar about it, as though he had seen it long ago. He continued to look at it, but was unable to bring the memory to the surface of his mind. He got the sense that he had stood here once before, about to inquire within for a room, but knew it to be impossible. Arkham did not exist, any more than Kingsport, or Innsmouth, or Dunwich. They were all creations of his imagination.

The absurdity of feeling the need to rent a room in an imaginary rooming house struck him with sudden force, and he giggled. A passing schoolgirl turned to stare at him with a curious expression. How long was it since he had last eaten? It was not a matter that he paid much attention to in his old body, but perhaps Monty's body was not as resilient. He resolved to see about finding a meal after he secured a room for the night.

It took three extended hammerings on the door before it opened to reveal a short, corpulent man with grey hair, fleshy wet lips, and a heavy beard stubble that was the same grey as the thinning hairs on his head. He had on a soiled white undershirt, over which hung the shoulder straps of a pair of canvas overalls that were strained by years of splashed paint, grease and dried plaster. He scratched his neck and regarded Lovecraft with suspicion.

"Do you have a room to rent?"

"No rooms. Go away."

Lovecraft caught the closing door and held it.

"Your sign says rooms to rent."

"All full, no rooms, go away."

The man's accent was Polish.

"Surely you have something. I'm very tired. I don't want to spend the entire morning searching for a room."

The man regarded him speculatively.

"One room on top floor."

"That's fine, I don't mind," Lovecraft assured him. "I'll take it."

The man stepped aside for Lovecraft to enter the hall and shut the door behind him, closing out the sounds of the street. Silently, he led the way up the steep flights of stairs. Several boarders regarded him with hostility as he passed their open doorways. They were all working class men and had a foreign look about them. The air smelled of boiled cabbage.

He was led to the end of the attic corridor and ushered into a fair-sized room with a single window. It contained a narrow bed with a cast-iron frame, a wooden chair and a rack on the wall for hanging clothes. In a corner stood a small table with an electric lamp. A naked light bulb hung on a frayed cord from the ceiling, which was oddly angled. It sloped down from one end of the room to the other. Lovecraft tried to think of some architectural feature he had seen on the outside of the venerable old house that would account for this irregularity. He noticed that one of the walls of the room was angled inward. Someone, presumably the previous tenant, had drawn lines of chalk on the angled wall and ceiling that converged on a single upper corner. On the bare floorboards a kind of pentacle had been inscribed with the same chalk, its sides congruent to various lines and numbers.

"You don't like room?"

"On the contrary, I like it very much," Lovecraft assured the man.

It had suddenly dawned on him why the house seemed so eerily familiar. He had written about it for one of his stories. It was the old witch-house, and the room in which he stood had once been the room of the notorious witch Keziah Mason. It could not have been chance alone that had led him to this place, of all places in Arkham. He realized the man was speaking to him.

"Your name, what your name, so I can write down in book."

Lovecraft introduced himself.

"I am Dombrowski," the landlord told him. "I collect rent, clean halls. No drinking, no women, no noise in night."

After collecting the first week's rent, Dombrowski left. Lovecraft listened to his heavy footfalls descend the flights of stairs before he closed the door.

He went to the chalk pentacle and studied it eagerly. He saw at once that the numbers upon and around it were from one to twenty-seven. Taking out the three parts of the key, he laid them carefully in the center of the pentacle and studied them. It could no more be a coincidence that the key bore the same numbers than his arrival at this house.

For three hours, he played with the number squares in his mind, arranging and rearranging them, turning them back to front, reflecting them left to right, and shuffling the levels. He sought to visualize with absolute clarity the magic cube they represented. He concentrated on the angled lines on the sloped ceiling and inclined northern wall that led to the corner of the room, trying to see them as glowing rays of fire in his imagination.

From time to time something scuttered inside the walls. He heard it knocking behind the baseboard and scratching across the ceiling. He tried to ignore the sound, but he could not resist picturing the creature that made the noises. It sounded so much like a rat, but he knew it was not a rat. Old Keziah Mason had possessed a familiar demon in the form of a small beast with the body of a rat, but the hands and face of a man. Lovecraft had no real doubt that it was Brown Jenkin moving inside the walls.

As night descended outside his window, he found himself exhausted both physically and mentally. Squares of numbers and angled lines danced in his head whenever he closed his eyes to rest them. Cursing in frustration, he sat on the bed and stared down at the pentacle. Nothing he had tried had made the least change in the room.

He lay back on the bed for a moment to think what he should do next. It was dark now, but both electric lights remained lit. As long as one of them glowed he would be safe from the shadow-walkers, even if they managed to sniff out his latest hiding place. He had some hope that he had eluded them, at least for the time being. If only Luther were here, he could no doubt solve the mathematical puzzle of the lines and numbers. Both he and Janice were probably dead by now, he thought. He would not abandon hope for them, but he saw no reason why the shadows or their terrible master should preserve their lives.

Without intending it, he closed his eyes, and almost at once drifted into a deep slumber.

20.

He found himself lying on his back in tall, browning grass. Sitting up, he gazed in wonder across the tips of the waving stalks, and realized that he sat in the midst of a flat grassland. The sun glowed red against the horizon. Was it morning or evening? He noticed frost on the dancing blades. Morning, then. The frosty air made him lightheaded, and he began to suspect that he was at some considerable elevation above sea level. The breeze cut through his thin shirt like knives of ice. It felt real enough. He pinched the back of his hand, then slapped his cheek several times. The sting was sharp and immediate.

Standing in the tall grass, which came up almost to his waist, he turned to survey the steppe, if that was what it was, and saw in the distance behind him an enclosure made of closely-joined black stone blocks with a gate set in the middle. Above the top of the wall, tiled roofs projected. Because it was the only structure in the grassland, he began to walk toward it. The frost-coated stalks crunched beneath his shoes. The compound was much further away than it at first seemed. As he walked, the sun rose behind him, but its rays held no warmth. From the corners of his eyes he caught movement in the grass. When he turned to look, it was always just the wind that made the blades rustle and bend. So why did he have such a strong impression of being watched?

The black wall of the enclosure towered enormously as he drew near. Each of its stones was the size of a city bus, and the double gate, iron-bound with great blackened timbers, was large enough to have admitted a ship under full sail. In one side of the gate there was a smaller door of more human dimensions. He tried the latch and it opened inward. He did not even think of knocking. Something in the chill air and the desolation of the high steppe whispered the need for silence.

Behind the gate extended a large open plaza paved with fieldstones. It was deserted. On the far side were large buildings that appeared to be the dormitories of a monastery, to judge by the gargoyles at their corners and the many grotesques carved in their walls. The windows of these buildings were shuttered. No smoke arose from the many chimneys. He stood still and listened, but heard no echo of a voice, no scuff of shoes against stone. The whole monastery complex held a deadness that would have been impossible to simulate.

In the center of the plaza stood a single-story building with a slate dome in the center of its flat roof. A circle of standing stones surrounded it, so weathered and ancient that it was impossible to determine if they were naturally formed or had been cut with tools. The walls of the little chapel inside the ring, if indeed it was a holy place, appeared to be made of the same black stone that formed the massive outer wall of the compound. Unlike the larger dormitory buildings behind, the chapel bore no fantastic decorations. In the center of its front was set a low arched door, but no windows broke its featureless walls. It looked incredibly ancient, as though the winds of aeons had rounded its corners.

From outside the fortification wall behind him came a distant howling. It was not quite like that of a dog, nor yet like that of a wolf. He had heard wolves sing at the zoo and knew their voice. Something was being hunted, but by what, his imagination refused to show him. He went back to the small door in the gate and closed it firmly. It latched shut from the inside, and he wondered why it had been left unlatched?

He approached the small chapel in the midst of the plaza with nervous steps. When its featureless door opened to his touch, he felt no surprise, only a kind of hopeless resignation. It was this way in nightmares. Events unfolded with an inevitable progression that could not be slowed or turned aside. Even though the dreamer knew of the doom that waited at the end of the path, he could not flee. He was himself a part of the nightmare, and could no more stop its unfolding than raindrops falling into a river could stop themselves from being swept downstream on the current.

The little black chapel was larger than he expected. He proceeded along a narrow corridor unbroken by doorways. Beams of morning light found their way in through narrow slots in the ceiling. It was enough to show him the way, but not enough to dispel the shadows. He wondered if the shadow-walkers had followed him from Arkham?

The corridor opened on a square chamber. Lovecraft would have judged it as large or larger than the chapel itself, but clearly that was impossible. It must only appear larger due to the lines of its architecture. However, it was a very convincing illusion.

The floor of this chamber lay at a level lower than the corridor. He descended six stairs and walked across it to stand at the edge of a circular well some twenty feet across. The opening in the floor lacked the protective barrier of a rim or lip. He stopped at its edge, but his eyes were not directed downward into its darkness. They gazed across the black gulf at a throne that occupied a dais on the far side of the room. Upon this throne, cloaked in shadow, sat a figure robed in saffron silk. The robe was embroidered in gold thread with chrysanthemums. Its hem concealed its wearer's feet. A silk veil covered the figure's face, and gloves of soft yellow leather hid its hands.

There was something vaguely disquieting about its posture. Lovecraft realized that its proportions were not quite correct, and the way it leaned expectantly forward had more of the great ape about it than anything human. He felt it watching him. The veil across its face rippled.

Despite its strangeness, there was also something familiar about the figure. He felt a strong sense of having seen it before, but like the maddeningly elusive details of a dream, he could not think when or where. Had he dreamed all this? Was he dreaming it now?

"I've come for the soul of Montague Willifred," Lovecraft said. He tried to make the words forceful but they quavered in his own ears.

Forcing his legs to carry him around the well on the left side, he approached the dais and mounted its five steps to stand directly in front of the throne, which he saw was covered in gold leaf, and decorated with golden oak leaves. The saffron-robed figure was larger than man-sized. Had it stood erect, it would have been a giant some seven or eight feet tall.

"I've come for the *Necronomicon*," Lovecraft said, this time with more conviction.

The yellow silk veil rippled. Through it he could see vague features, but there was not enough background light in the chamber to render the veil fully transparent.

Moved by he knew not what impulse, Lovecraft reached out and snatched the veil away. Instantly, the yellow robe collapsed onto the throne. He felt the pile of fabric frantically, but it was empty, and chill to the touch. Whatever had given it form had vanished as quickly and completely as a popped soap bubble. The coolness of the cloth disquieted him the most. It should retain the warmth from the body of whatever had worn it, but it felt as though it had just been lifted out of an icebox.

Gathering up the robe, he threw it to one side and sat upon the throne. It was done on impulse. His mind and body were weary of jumping with fear at every incident. Sitting on the throne was an act of defiance, a way of informing his unseen watcher that he no longer cared what happened to him. As he sat, he drifted into a kind of dreaming revere. Time passed, but how much time he could not estimate. It felt like centuries. It was the music that brought him back to himself. He heard it dimly, as though it echoed up the shaft of the well—the insane nasal droning of reed flutes and the twang of plucked strings.

Lovecraft shook himself awake and bent his head to listen. The music stopped. He blinked and looked about the chamber. The rising sun had managed to work its way through chinks in the dome on the roof, and now shone directly downward into the well. By its rays he saw that a spiral staircase of stone blocks extended from the sides of the well, winding down into the deeper darkness.

For a time, he continued to sit, but at last he got up from his seat and began the long and treacherous descent.

21.

The stones projecting from the side of the well were no more than three feet across, those that were not broken, and many had corners or ends missing. A few were almost entirely broken away, forcing him to step across the gap. Fortunately, his eyes were not long adjusting to the dim light. It showed the steps as oblongs of grey against the blackness of the gulf below. The stair spiralled in an anticlockwise direction. He trailed the fingertips of his right hand against the damp, cool stones on the inner side of the well.

The stair seemed endless. He lost all measure of time. He knew he had been creeping downward for hours by the weariness in his thighs, but whether two hours or twenty, he could not have told. At some point he realized that the well was widening. It was the echoes of his shoes striking the stone steps that made him aware of the change in its diameter. The interval of the echo grew longer and longer, until at last the echo ceased. The slope of the wall was so gradual, he would never otherwise have guessed its existence. The light illuminated only the area immediately around him—it did not show the far side of the well.

The widening of its walls indicated that well was not, as he would have supposed, a cylinder, but a cone. Once he became aware of this, he could not help but sense the vastness of the black space into which he tip-toed, feeling for each step before taking it. There was movement in the air, vagrant puffs of wind, and the soft beating of great wings, but peer as he would into the darkness, he never saw the source. The breeze passed and re-passed him, caressing him almost as would a lover. His imagination began to paint images of what the winged creatures might look like, each more terrifying than the last. He half-expected his head to be snipped from his shoulders by some monstrous beak.

When he reached the bottom of the well, it was an anticlimax. Suddenly there were no more stairs. Instead, he found himself on a walkway some ten feet broad that ran around the side of the well. At the inner edge of this perimeter walkway, no more than a few inches below its surface, the well was filled with black water. It was almost impossible to see by the dim light where the stones of the walkway ended and the water began, but he knelt down and felt for the edge with his hands until his fingers dipped into the icy water.

Sudden overwhelming thirst twisted his stomach and constricted his throat. He cupped his hands in the water and lifted it to his lips. Only the thought of what the water might contain kept him from drinking. After an internal struggle, he cursed and dashed the water back down. The splash was answered by a louder splash further out across the unseen lake. Something lived in the water. He realized that he might be in danger by staying in one spot at its edge, and forced himself up on weary legs. He began to trace around the walkway, his right hand on the wall, continuing in the same direction as the stair.

After an interminable length of time, he came upon a small opening in the wall. Here was a decision. Did he stay beside the water, where there was at least some trace of light, and perhaps creatures he could eat to sustain his life, or did he take this new course? For a time the effort to choose paralysed him. Finally, it was the sense of being guided that allowed him to overcome this indecision and turn resolutely into the passage.

It began well enough as a tunnel some eight feet or so high and five feet wide. After the first dozen steps into it, he could not see anything. He had never known so complete a blackness. It was like being totally blind. He was comforted by the sound of his footfalls. By brushing his fingers on both walls, he was able to assure himself that there were no side-branchings.

The passage did not remain straight and level. He was first conscious that the floor tilted downward. For a way, it became steep enough that he feared he would lose his footing and slide down its length. Then it gradually levelled and began to ascend. At the same time he thought he detected the passage bending first to the left, then to the right, and back again, but this bending was gentle enough that he could not be certain about it.

None of this alarmed him greatly, but when the passage started to constrict, he felt apprehension and a sense of oppression on his chest. It narrowed until its sides brushed his shoulders, and the ceiling lowered so much that he found himself bending his back and knees. There came a point when he was forced to drop to his hands and knees and crawl forward with the ceiling of the passage brushing down on his arched back. He had never suffered in a particular way from claustrophobia, but he found his inner panic growing.

He reached a wall at the end of this constricted passage, and felt over it frantically. There was a hole through it that was not much wider than his shoulders. He reached into it as far as he could reach, but felt only smooth stone on either side. For a long while he crouched on his hands and knees, unable to force himself to squirm into the hole. What if it angled downward and he began to slide? What if it continued to constrict? His mental balance teetered on the brink of hysteria, and he found himself fighting to hold back a wordless scream of sheer terror.

It was the memory of what lay behind him, of what he had come through, that finally make him extend his arms into the hole and wriggle forward. There was no going back for him. If by some miracle he found a way back to Arkham, or even to Providence, the shadow-walkers and their master would still be hunting him.

After a mercifully brief distance, the hole opened into a chamber. With great relief he slid himself onto the stone floor of this lightless place and lay there, completely drenched in his own sweat. It was not the sweat of exertion, but of rank fear. He lay face down on the stone, feeling and listening to the thunder of his heartbeats as their intervals began to lengthen, and the beats approached a more normal pace.

When he regained some measure of mental poise, Lovecraft pushed himself wearily to his feet and felt around the perimeter of the chamber. He found that it was no more than ten or twelve feet across. The ceiling was high enough that he could not touch it, even when he jumped upward. Directly opposite the hole through which he had crawled, a recess in the wall held a small wooden door. It was made of stout planks and ironwork, and it appeared to be bolted on the other side. He spent five futile minutes tugging on the ring that served as its handle, rattling the heavy door against its bolt, before he was able to accept that he would never be able to force it open.

This final setback, mundane as it was, broke whatever reserve remained to him. He allowed himself to slide down to a sitting posture on the floor with his back against the locked portal, and began to weep silently. Hot tears rolled freely down both cheeks. Periodically, he wiped them away with his fingers, but they continued to pour from his eyes in a seemingly endless flow. He did not sob. He found that he didn't even feel sadness. He felt empty inside. The tears rolled forth with a life of their own, completely beyond his comprehension or control.

22.

In the perfect blackness, the absolute silence, he heard a faint tinkling. Wiping his tears away on the cuffs of his shirt, he held his breath to listen. There it was again, the sound of metal striking glass, but where did it originate? His ears, or rather Monty's ears, were good, but even so it took him some time to trace the tinkling to the center of the round chamber. By touch he discovered that there was nothing on the floor but a paving stone, about the size and thickness of a city manhole cover. He realized that the noise came from beneath this stone, and with a sudden burst of strength, forced the stone aside. Panting from the effort, he felt around in the darkness.

Beneath where the stone had rested he found a recess in the floor. He traced its circular edge, but hesitated to put his hands into its depths. The thought crossed his mind that it might contain scorpions, or snakes, or God knows what other horrors. There was only one way to discover what the hole contained, that he knew well enough, but still it took him many minutes to work up the courage to thrust his hands downward.

In the center of what proved to be a shallow depression, his fumbling fingers located a glass bottle with a wax-sealed cork stopper closing its broad mouth. Intricate mouldings covered the sides of the glass, the exact shapes of which his groping fingertips could not determine.

As he moved the bottle, something tinkled inside it. Lovecraft realized that it must be similar to the soul bottles he had seen on the long table in the house of the terrible old man of Kingsport. The tinkling came from a lead weight suspended on the end of a silk thread. As the bottle moved, the weight struck the side. But the bottle had tinkled before he had even touched it. Was it possible that it contained a soul?

His time in the old man's house had not been wasted. The old man had shown him many wonders, among them how to interpret the tinkling of the lead weights against the sides of his bottles. The trick, he told Lovecraft, was to open his mind and to let his thoughts wander and become abstracted. When there was a stillness in his mind, the tinkling of the lead would form intelligible words. So the old man claimed.

Lovecraft had not had time to experiment with the method at the old man's house, but what did he have at his disposal here, in this dark place, other than time? He sat on the floor cross-legged, the bottle cradled close to his groin, and let his mind wander. As vagrant thoughts arose, he began to still them one by one. Of its own volition, the lead weight in the bottle started to strike its side, making a continuous but varied tinkling sound that he could not only hear, but feel as vibrations through his hands and thighs.

After a time, he found himself asking a question over and over in his mind. He framed it softly with his lips.

"Who are you?"

To his surprise, he understood the tinkling of the lead. It spoke a name.

"Montague Willifred."

A great sense of relief washed through Lovecraft and left him weak. He had found the soul of the man he had sought for so long.

"Take heart, Monty," he murmured. "I've come to rescue you from your prison and take you home." As he spoke these hollow words he looked around at the darkness.

"Who are you?" the bottle tinkled.

"I'm the man you called into your body, when your soul was stolen from it."

The lead struck the bottle with a confused rattling in which Lovecraft could distinguish no words.

"Calm down, Monty. Did you not call my soul into your body?"

After a few minutes, the tinkling became purposeful again.

"Am I not in my own body?"

"No, you are not," Lovecraft told him, perplexed. It seemed Monty did not even know what had happened to him.

"Then, where?" the bottle asked.

As concisely as he could express it, Lovecraft told Monty what had become of him. The bottle was silent so long that he began to think the shock had incapacitated the soul trapped within it. At last, the lead weight began to strike the glass. It was a string of blasphemies and obscenities the like of which only the terrible old man could have surpassed. So forcefully did the lead dance against the glass, he wondered if it were possible that it might break the bottle. After a time the frantic motion became more regular.

"Again, who are you?"

"I thought you knew," Lovecraft told him, his heart filled with pity for the young man. "I am Howard Phillips Lovecraft, the writer, of Providence, Rhode Island."

Again there was a long pause as Monty digested this information.

"It is a great honour to at last speak with you," the bottle tinkled.

"I am delighted to make your acquaintance," Lovecraft said. "I only wish the circumstances were more conducive to social intercourse."

"I am your great-grandson."

"So Janice informed me."

"I have always worshipped your work, and you, its creator."

"That's gratifying to hear. I had always supposed that nobody cared enough about my stories to even remember them."

"In my time period you are recognized as one of the greatest American writers."

Lovecraft considered this effusive praise soberly. The young man's obsession with him was of little help in their current predicament.

"What do you know of your present circumstances?"

"Only what you have told me," the lead tinkled. "The last thing I remember is fighting for my life in my house. Two of my friends attacked me. Then I woke up in this dark place. I can't see anything. I can't move, or even feel my body. I guess that's because I don't have a body."

The bottle made a frantic tinkling from which Lovecraft was unable to extract any words. Finally, he realized it was Monty laughing. It continued so long, Lovecraft finally spoke, if only to interrupt it. He feared for the sanity of the disembodied soul.

"Let me explain to you what has been happening while you have been unconscious."

The tinkling stopped, as Lovecraft had hoped it would. He spoke at length, explaining how he had gone to sleep in his bed at Jane Brown Memorial Hospital, only to awaken in a straitjacket in Butler

Hospital, the prisoner not only of an insane asylum, but of another man's flesh. He told of Janice's rescue, and the attack by the shadow-walkers on Monty's mansion, his flight with Janice and Luther through the dimensional portal to the island in the Miskatonic River, then of the events in Arkham, and how the three of them had followed up on the scraps of information they had discovered at Monty's dorm room. When he reached the point at which Luther and Janice were abducted from Seaton Hall by the shadows, the bottle began to tinkle.

"Were they injured? Is Janice still alive?"

"That I have no way to know," Lovecraft admitted. "I hold hope that both of them were kept alive, but it is hope unsupported by any evidence."

"He is always one step ahead of us," the bottle tinkled. "He taunts and torments us for his own amusement."

"Who?" Lovecraft asked, but he already knew the answer.

"Nyarlathotep," the bottle tinkled.

"But I created Nyarlathotep," Lovecraft said. "He is no more than a figment of my imagination."

"You're wrong about that," Monty said. "You didn't create the things you wrote about in your stories, you caught glimpses in your dreams of an alternate reality, and of some of the creatures who inhabit it."

"Can such an abomination exist on any plane of being?"

"He exists," Monty assured him. "To our limited minds he appears wholly evil, but he transcends the petty dualities of humanity."

"Why has he persecuted you and your coven?"

"I can only guess. In part it is because I sought to obtain the *Necronomicon*. He guards the book from humanity so that we will never know its full power. Those who delve too deeply in its pages he makes raving mad. It's not the book that causes madness, but its secret guardian. But there is something else in his malice. I sense it. He hates me and takes delight in punishing me. I don't know why."

"Why are you so determined to obtain the *Necronomicon*?"

"To bring you back, of course," the bottle tinkled. Lovecraft was not certain he had interpreted the lead correctly.

"I don't understand."

"All my life, I've been obsessed with you and your work. I knew you were an ancestor of mine, and you were my hero, or maybe I should be honest and say you were my god. It always seemed such a tragedy that so towering a genius was cut from life at so early an age. I decided to correct the wrong that was done to you by fate."

Lovecraft digested this confusing speech for a time, but it did not clarify itself.

"I still don't quite understand what you mean."

The tinkling laughter came, this time with more control than before.

"I formed the Lovecraft coven for one purpose—to find a way to restore you to life, so that you could continue to create. That's why I looked for the *Necronomicon*. I need the book to complete the ritual of your restoration."

Lovecraft had always been an atheist, even in early childhood, but there was something about this casual admission that chilled him. It was blasphemous on a level that went far beyond ordinary acts of spiritual desecration.

"You were trying to resurrect me? Did you mean for me to take over your body?"

No, no," the bottle tinkled. "In your own body, cured of your disease."

"Is that even possible?"

"It is, or at least it would have been, had I been able to obtain a true copy of the *Necronomicon*. But I was blocked and frustrated at every turn."

Lovecraft remained silent for a time, thinking about this information. His legs were becoming numb from sitting in the same position for so long. He shifted stiffly to ease them. He started to look around, but what was the point? The darkness remained absolute.

"Monty, answer me this," he asked with hesitation. "If I smash this bottle, will that free your soul?"

The answer did not come immediately.

"Yes. But it would expel your soul from my body."

"What would happen to my soul? Would I find myself back in Brown Hospital at Providence?"

"Unlikely. From what you've told me, you entered my body after the death of your own. I'm sorry, H. P., but you've got nothing to go back to."

Nothing to go back to. Lovecraft allowed the words to repeat themselves in his mind. It was the same thing he had been thinking since this fantastic episode began. There was no use trying to retrace his steps because he had nothing to go back to.

Even so, he thought, Monty deserves something better than this. He hefted the weight of the bottle in his hands. What did it matter if he died? He was dead already. At least he could return the young man—his great-grandson—to his own flesh. Slowly he raised the bottle above his head.

But would that really be merciful? Monty would find himself alone in this black prison, with no way to advance. Maybe he was better off as a disembodied soul, at least until his body was freed from this prison. Then there was Janice and Luther to think about. As long as he remained alive, he could pursue their rescue, no matter how hopeless the task might seem. Once he smashed the bottle, he would descend to oblivion, or worse, become a revenant, where he could do no good for any of the others, and no good for himself. There had to be a reason why he had been snatched out of his dying shell and thrust into Monty's flesh. He lowered the bottle more carefully than he had raised it.

"When I break this bottle, will your soul go back into this body?"

"Probably. Almost certainly. But the shock may kill me."

"Do you mean that when I break the bottle, I may kill us both?"

"That's my guess about what would happen, but I can't be sure of anything. This is all uncharted territory."

Lovecraft lapsed into silent brooding. There seemed no good option. At last he was forced by physical discomfort to move. He climbed to his feet, the bottle under one arm, and realized that his legs had fallen asleep. He flexed them and waited for the pins and needles to pass. The bottle began to tinkle.

"What are you going to do?"

"As long as we remain trapped in this cell, there's nothing I can do," Lovecraft murmured.

Even as he uttered these words, the loud metallic clank of a bolt sliding back in its guide broke the dead silence like a clap of thunder. It could only be the bolt that secured the door. Lovecraft tensed and prepared himself for an attack in the darkness. A soft chuckle reached his ears, so low that he was not sure whether he had heard it, or only imagined it. He waited, but no other sound came.

23.

Feeling around the circular wall of the chamber, he reached the small wooden door and pushed against it. The door opened without complaint. Oil lamps suspended from the ceiling on chains illuminated the passage beyond. Lovecraft passed through with care, watchful for any pitfall. The floor of the passage sloped downward. He saw no joints in the walls. The passage had been cut from solid rock.

The lead in the bottle tinkled.

"We're in a passage that goes deeper under the monastery," he murmured.

For the first time he had light by which to study the bottle. The glass was unusually thick and irregular, smoky with impurities and of a greenish hue. All over its surface were what appeared to be red occult symbols that had been cast into the glass during its creation. He stood near a lamp and studied the bottle. The symbols were made of thin lines of a ruby glass that had been dribbled over the bottle while it was still molten, so that the red and green glasses had bonded together. The wax that covered the cork stopper was such a dark red that it was almost black, and had a strange odour that turned his stomach when he raised it to his nose.

This time there was no trick, no ordeal. The passage simply ended on a door very similar to the one he had passed through to escape the round chamber. He reached out and pushed against it, certain that it would be bolted. To his surprise, it opened as easily as the first door.

The well-lit square room beyond had been carved from the solid bedrock in the same way as the passage, but in the form of an enclosed amphitheatre. An upper walkway some ten feet across wrapped around the four walls of the large chamber. The central part of the floor, some six feet lower than this walkway, was accessed by stairs that ran continuously around the room on all four sides. In the middle of this lower area stood an oblong stone table that had the appearance of a pagan altar. On it rested a large black book beneath a canopy of leaded glass that had the shape of a little house.

These things Lovecraft noticed with a part of his mind, but most of his attention went immediately to the two figures chained to opposite walls at the higher level of the room, so that they looked down upon the black altar and the book. To his left, as he stepped through the doorway, was Janice, and to his right, Luther. Both were held upright with their backs to the walls, their arms extended apart by chains that bound their wrists. Their ankles were not chained. All this he noticed in the instant it took him to enter the amphitheatre.

"Yours is a face I never expected to see again," Luther said with a wry smile. His voice sounded dry.

"We thought the shadow-walkers had killed you," Janice said.

"I feared the same of you," Lovecraft admitted. "Have you been hurt?"

Janice shook her head.

"We woke up chained to these walls. The pain in my shoulders woke me up. We haven't seen anyone but you."

"This whole monastery seems deserted," Lovecraft said.

"What's that under your arm?" Luther asked.

Lovecraft advanced slowly down the stairs to the lower level and approached the altar.

"This is Monty. Say hello to your friends, Monty."

The lead tinkled against the glass.

"You have got to be shitting me," Luther said. "Monty's in there?"

"He is indeed."

"Well, how do we get him out?"

Lovecraft set the bottle down on the altar beside the glass canopy and regarded the book beneath it. It was a large book of several hundred parchment leaves bound in black leather that was somewhat worm-riddled and rat-gnawed at the corners, where the metal brackets had not protected it. They were of brass and coated with verdigris. The leather had been cunningly worked using a technique known as blind-stamping, whereby lines and other ornamentations are impressed into it without the benefit of gold leaf. The decoration was tastefully done and gave no hint as to what the book contained.

"Can this be—?"

"We can't think what else it can be," Luther said.

"But why?"

"I think it was put there to torment us," Janice said. "The coven sought access to it for so many months without success, and now here it is, so close, yet still out of reach."

"Would Nyar—would *he* do something so petty?" Lovecraft asked.

"It may not be petty," Luther said. "Everything he does, he does for a reason, but that reason is not always clear to us. What to us may seem spiteful may for him have a higher purpose we can never understand."

Lovecraft mounted the steps to where Janice stood chained and examined the iron bands around her wrists. They were locked into place with a keyed mechanism, too tight for her to slip her hands through, and much too thick to break. The chains were anchored firmly to heavy rods set deep in the stone wall.

"I can't free you without tools," he said at last.

"You can't free us, but maybe you can free yourself," Janice said with sudden excitement, staring across at Luther. "And Monty at the same time."

"That's right," Luther agreed. "The coven was working on the necromantic ritual to bring you back in your own body. We pieced it together from a dozen different ancient sources until it was almost complete, but we never had the *Necronomicon* where the actual incantation is written. That was the last piece of the puzzle."

Lovecraft turned in a complete circle, staring about the enclosed amphitheatre with unease. He had a sense of being watched, but there was no one at the door, which stood open to the passage. He descended the stairs to the altar.

"If this ritual were to work, I would appear in my former body alive and well?"

"That's the idea," Luther said with a shrug. "We won't know until we try it."

"And that means my soul, or consciousness, or whatever inhabits this body, would leave it?"

"It will create a vacuum in Monty's body that may draw his soul back into it," Janice told him.

"Or his body may simply drop dead," Lovecraft said.

She met his gaze with an unhappy expression, then nodded.

"With your soul in Monty's body, and Monty's soul in the bottle, there are too many variables to predict what will occur," Luther said. "But we have the book. At least it's something we can try."

The green glass bottle tinkled on the altar. Lovecraft stood beside it and closed his eyes, calming his mind.

"Say that again, if you would, Monty."

Again the bottle tinkled. Lovecraft nodded.

"Monty expresses his willingness to try the ritual."

The three of them couched Lovecraft through the ritual of necromancy. What details Janice and Luther forgot, Monty supplied from his glass prison. Its simplicity surprised Lovecraft. There was no need to draw a complex pentacle on the floor, which was just as well since none of them possessed a pen or pencil. The main requirement was the visualization of various geometric patterns. These Lovecraft drew upon the air with his index finger toward the four walls of the room, which for ritual purposes represented the four cardinal directions. As he shaped each sign, he uttered the names he was told to speak. In life, his memory had always been near to what is called a photographic memory. It served him well now in avoiding errors in the sequence of the signs and names he was required to impress upon the aether.

He walked widdershins around the altar to define a magic circle. The direction of the circle disquieted him, although he said nothing. It was anticlockwise, or against the direction of solar movement across the heavens. The witch covens of old Europe had danced widdershins during their sabbats, or so the inquisitors claimed. He had read of it in Cotton Mather's books, where it was declared an abomination.

"It's time for the incantation," Janice said, watching him closely. "Hurry, before the seals fade from the astral matrix."

Lovecraft approached the altar slab, conscious of the ritual circle flickering with green fire in the air all around it. The circle was actually visible to his sight from the corners of his eyes, along with the redly glowing symbols at the four quarters of space.

"Smash the canopy," Janice told him, her voice trembling with excitement. "Turn to page ninety-three and read the incantation you find there. You won't understand the words. It's in a lost language."

"I thought the incantation was on page two hundred and twenty-one," Luther said.

"No, that's what we thought at first, but later research revealed the true location."

Lovecraft tried to lift the leaded glass canopy off the book, and discovered that it had been fixed into the surface of the black stone altar with plugs of molten lead. He used his elbow to break out the roof panels of the little glass house, and extracted the book through the hole, shaking off the shards of glass. The book was astonishingly heavy. It required the main part of his strength to cradle it on his left arm and open it to page ninety-three. Fortunately, the pages were numbered in the upper corners.

The leather of the cover felt warm against his palm where he supported it, and the parchment leaves seemed to slide through his fingers as though alive. The book almost opened itself to the correct page, in the center of which was a block of text in antique black letter. Lovecraft was familiar with black letter from his childhood study of old books in his grandfather's library. It took some getting used to, particularly a few of the capital letters, which were easy to confuse with one another.

"Read it, now!" Janice said. "What are you waiting for?"

He began to read the unintelligible words of the alien language, which sounded harsh in his throat as he formed them. The tinkling of the lead in the green bottle became frantic. In his concentration on projecting the details of the ritual into the astral matrix, Lovecraft had nearly forgotten Monty. What was he saying now? It was a poor time to start a conversation, Lovecraft thought with irritation.

"What's he saying?" Luther asked.

"It doesn't matter," Janice snapped at him with annoyance. "The ritual can't be paused, it has to be completed."

"I can't quite make him out," Lovecraft admitted as he inclined his ear to the bottle. There's a kind of roaring in my head."

"It's the ritual," Janice said. "Don't worry about it."

"He's saying something about a number. He keeps repeating the number two-two-one. Wasn't that the number you said, Luther?"

"I was sure that was the page for the incantation," Luther told him.

"For fuck's sake, get on with it," Janice said. "You fools are going to ruin everything."

Lovecraft looked at her in surprise. She seemed strangely agitated. Probably it was nothing more than her concern for Monty and the uncertainty over the outcome of the ritual.

The frantic tinkling of the lead weight inside the green bottle changed its cadence.

"Trick? What trick, Monty? Slow down, I can't understand you."

"Howard," Luther said in a hollow voice. "I'm almost certain you've got the wrong page in the book."

Lovecraft glanced at him. Luther's face was pale, and he was staring, not at the altar, but across the room at Janice. He turned his head, and saw why. She was cloaked in shadow that slid along her limbs and seemed to distort their shapes. On the underside of her arms and chin there was a kind of dull red glow, like that of embers in the fireplace that are covered with ash but still glow through it. Her face shifted and changed as he looked at it, never the same for more than an instant.

Her black eyes glared at him with pure fury, and she spoke in a voice that was too deep and harsh for a human throat.

"Read the fucking incantation now, or I'll kill you all."

24.

Janice spread her arms wide with an expression of idiot joy. The iron bands around her wrists glowed red, then orange, then suddenly flared blue-white with such intensity that Lovecraft had to shield his eyes with his hand. The chains fell off her and hung down the wall, swinging from side to side and dripping molten iron.

She stepped forward and looked down at Lovecraft with an expression of mingled hatred and contempt. Her face continued to distort like the image in a carnival mirror, transitioning from feminine to masculine to bestial and back again in a matter of moments. Heat rising from her body made the air in front of her ripple, and Lovecraft saw wisps of smoke curl up from her clothing.

"That's not Janice," Luther said.

"You never were very bright, except in mathematics," she said without looking at him. Her gaze never left Lovecraft.

"You planned all this from the first," Lovecraft said.

"Obviously."

"When did you take over Janice's body?"

The sound of her laughter was disturbing.

"You humans are so fucking stupid. There is no Janice. There never was a Janice."

"That means you've been planning this for years," Lovecraft said, his mind racing.

"For more years than you can imagine. Now read the incantation and get this over with."

"Not until you explain its purpose."

She stomped her foot on the floor, and the stone cracked beneath it. He felt the vibration through the soles of his feet. The green bottle on the altar tinkled frantically.

"Mortal, you could no more comprehend my purpose than a cockroach could learn to solve quadratic equations. You are wasting my time, and what is more pertinent, from your point of view, you are pissing me off."

Lovecraft bent his head, listening hard. He leafed through the book until he found page two hundred and twenty-one.

"If we're so unimportant, why did you even need our help?" Luther asked.

"A reasonable question, and for that, I will answer it. Not all you worms are the same. Some of you have powers of which you remain ignorant your entire brief lives, and some of those powers can be used to bend certain laws that are otherwise impregnable. Lovecraft is such a worm. My little glow worm, glowing so brightly in the higher planes but with his light barely suspected on the hellish level you call your reality. Suffice it to say that I need this mortal to read the incantation specified, in this place, at this time, so that by vocalizing it, his mind will shape certain geometric patterns and proportions in a specific sequence."

She returned her attention to Lovecraft, who all this while had continued to murmur under his breath, his eyes on the book.

"Do you think I'm toying with you? Turn back to page ninety-three and read!"

He ignored her.

"I can blast the flesh from your bones as easily as I raise my hand."

"If you kill me, who will read the passage?"

She stalked down the steps to the lower level, her legs strangely stiff and her footfalls flat. The leather pants and blouse she wore began to catch fire and fall away from her limbs in blazing clots. When she tried to advance further, the almost invisible magic circle he had projected around the altar glowed a bright gold, and she stopped and stood grinding her teeth, the roots of which seeped blood over her writhing lips.

"I don't need to kill you, only to hurt you."

"She can't cross the circle," Luther told Lovecraft.

Lovecraft ignored her. He had to hold his concentration on the text to avoid mispronouncing the words, which he was forced to form and sound phonetically since the language was alien to him. One word he recognized—the name Yog-Sothoth. As he spoke the name, the thing that had been Janice lunged forward with her arms raised and her fingers spread like claws, but she seemed to rebound from the empty air and stood leaning in that posture no more than four feet away from Lovecraft, as though about to embrace him.

"Give me what I want, and I will set Monty free and return him to his flesh. I will resurrect your corpse and cure your cancer. I will give the three of you wealth and power."

Lovecraft stopped speaking and looked at her. He seemed to consider. The green bottle on the altar began to tinkle.

"Don't listen, Howard. She's lying," Luther said.

"Meddling asshole, I've had enough of you."

She raised one blackened hand, and abruptly clenched her fingers into a fist. Lovecraft heard a sickening wet crunch behind him, and forced himself to look over his shoulder. Where Luther had once stood, there hung from the chains a bloody and dripping mass of raw red meat. There was nothing human left in its shape. He looked back at her. She snapped her blackened teeth at him until they broke, her tongue flickering between them like the tongue of a snake.

"Is that what you intend for me?"

"Oh no. I intend far worse for you. Now do as I say!"

He set the book down on the altar and took up a shard of glass from the shattered canopy. Calmly, he began to cut a symbol into the palm of his left hand. He did not know how deep it had to be, so he cut it deeper than he thought was necessary, to be safe. With blood streaming from his left palm, he cut a similar but inverted symbol into his right palm.

"What are you doing? Are you completely insane?"

"Tell me what to do."

"You'll do as you're told, that's what you'll do, or you'll spend the rest of eternity screaming."

"Tell me what to do next."

The lead in the bottle continued to tinkle with frantic haste.

She turned her head, and for the first time seemed to notice the bottle.

"So that's how it is? Well, I can put a stop to that."

Lovecraft tried to ignore her, no easy task with her horrible burning caricature of a face hanging no more than a few feet away from his own. He raised his bloody hands into the air in a gesture of invocation and spoke three times the name Monty had told him to speak.

"Yog-Sothoth! Yog-Sothoth! Yog-Sothoth!"

Nothing happened. Lovecraft felt the heart in his chest trip over itself, so intense was the failure of anticipation. The Janice-thing screamed with triumph, and the magic circle around the altar flickered out.

At the instant of its failure, her shape transformed from that of a burning hag into something his mind refused to comprehend. Where she had stood there remained only a kind of grey, flickering blind spot. He saw nothing when he looked at it, but from its irregular edges appendages projected. They were serpentine and covered with black hooks. On their ends black claws snapped open and shut.

The cable-like projections lashed down upon the altar before he could even flinch. Some of them clutched the book and drew it into the air, slamming it shut in the process. Others coiled around the green glass bottle and yanked it away. He heard the forlorn tinkle of the lead inside it just before the abomination dashed it down upon the stones of the floor, shattering it into ten thousand fragments.

As the hooked and barbed black cables darted down toward his face from either side of the zone of nothingness that hid its true form, Lovecraft clapped his bloody hands together above his head, palm to palm. They touched, and the ceiling of the room split open to the heavens, allowing blinding white light that was filled with iridescent, transparent coloured spheres to surround and enfold his body. He felt the spheres penetrate his skin and flesh and bone like a soothing balm, and sensed at the same time an agonized howl of frustration from the blind spot. The brightness thrust it away an infinite distance with the ease of the autumn breeze blowing away a dried leaf from a branch.

Is this death? Lovecraft thought.

Into his mind there came surprise, and then a gentle amusement. It was like the smile of an indulgent father when his infant son says something at once ridiculous yet charming in its naïveté.

25.

Howard awoke in his bed with morning sunlight streaming across the pillow and over his shining golden curls. He clenched his tiny fists and screwed them into his eyes to rub away the sleep, then stretched and rolled to his side.

The Irish maid came into his room with an armload of freshly laundered clothes and began to put them away into his bureau. She glanced at him over her shoulder.

"Time to get up, young master," she said. "Your mother is holding breakfast for you."

Howard liked her because she talked in a funny way that always made him laugh. And she was pretty, another reason to like her. He looked at the plaster ceiling, blinking sleepily.

"I had the strangest dream, Bridget."

"You always have strange dreams," she chided.

"No, this one was really weird."

She slid the bottom drawer of the bureau shut and came to sit on the edge of the bed with an indulgent expression.

"Tell me about it, then."

"It was all about . . . all about . . . this house that had black shadows coming through the walls, and, and . . . I wasn't even in my own body . . . and I went through this doorway to another city . . ."

She waited expectantly. Howard was always telling her his dreams.

"Go on, then, what else."

He frowned, his brow wrinkling over the bridge of his nose.

"That's all I remember. It's all gone now, but it was so real."

"There, there, never mind. Maybe it will come back to you and you can write it down in your journal."

Howard pouted. He had wanted to tell her the entire dream, but he could remember none of it.

"Why do we forget our dreams, Bridget?"

"Back home they say if we didn't forget our dreams, we'd all go mad."

"But I want to remember them. I want to remember all of them."

She slid her hand under the quilt and slapped him smartly on the buttocks through his pyjama bottoms.

"Right now you're late for breakfast. Do you want to go down yourself, or do you want me to carry you?"

He giggled and slide out of bed on the opposite side. She pretended to try to catch him as he ran around the foot and down the upper hallway.

"Don't run," his grandfather said sternly through the open door of his upstairs sitting room.

Howard slid to a stop on the hall runner and put his head around the doorjamb.

"Good-morning, grandfather."

"It is a good morning, Howard. Very good indeed."

He sat in a comfortable armchair, reading the newspaper, his grey hair illuminated by the sunlight that found its way through the lace curtains. Looking at the old man's carefree, smiling face, Howard felt a deep sense of mingled love and belonging. Grandfather Phillips was the center of his world, the axis around which the entire household revolved.

"Did your stocks go up?"

The old man smiled more broadly and nodded.

"They went up, and up, and up!"

He threw the newspaper into the air so that its sheets drifted down separately across the carpet. Lovecraft ran into the room.

"Are we wealthy, grandfather?"

The old man motioned him over to the chair and lifted the boy onto his knee. Howard's golden curls caught the same ray of sunlight that illuminated his own head.

"Just between us men," he whispered into the boy's ear, "business has been good."

Howard slid from the old man's knee. He picked up a sheet of newspaper and threw it over his head in imitation of his grandfather, screaming like a wild Indian.

"Now get down to breakfast before your mother sends out a search party."

The boy raced from the sitting room, not heeding the old man's command to slow down, and ran at full speed down the stair and across the hall into the dining room, where his mother sat at the head of the table in her white morning dress. She had just finished her eggs and toast.

"Come over here, let me look at you," she ordered.

He skipped across the hardwood floor and stood beside her chair, suffering her to tilt his face to the light from the window. She peeled up each eyelid, and opened his mouth to peer in at his tongue.

"Are you sure you feel quite well?"

"I feel wonderful," Howard said. He jumped into the air. "See?"

"Eat your breakfast, then, before it gets cold."

He perched on the edge of the chair that had been set for him at her elbow. A maid came forward and removed the warming cover from his plate. It was eggs and sausage, with toast. He ate with a good appetite and sipped from the glass of orange juice beside the plate as he chewed.

"What are you going to do today, my darling boy?"

Lovecraft waved his fork vaguely toward the back of the house.

"I have to build my railroad. The coachman is helping me lay the track, and I've got ever so much to do. Stations to build, and towns, and bridges."

"That does sound like a busy day," his mother said with a smile.

Howard looked at her, and realized that she was beautiful.

"Now don't take up all of Mr. Kelly's time. He has other work to do, you know."

"I won't. I'm a big boy now. I can do most of it myself."

"You are a big boy," she said with a trace of wistfulness. "Soon you'll be all grown up."

"I don't want to grow up," he said, head down as he sawed at his sausage. The effort made his halo of golden ringlets dance.

"Howard! That's a strange thing to say."

"I mean it. I don't want things to change. Everything is perfect just the way it is. I wish it could be this way for ever and ever and ever."

A shadow passed slowly across the window, darkening the dining room. In a moment it was gone, and the sun shone in as brightly as before. His mother looked at the window, then back at him.

"What ever do you suppose that was?"

"I know what it was," Howard said. "It was in my dream. It was . . . it was . . ."

But try as he would, he could not quite remember.

Iron Chain

1.

It came as no surprise to Nick Hanford when his paternal grandfather left him money in his will. The old man had always liked him. After his father passed away from prostate cancer when Nick was twelve, he had come to look upon crusty Papa Joe as a second father. They saw each other less and less as the years passed, but they always kept in touch, and the affection of the old man did not diminish.

The surprise was the amount. A few words from the balding family lawyer in a Dickensian office that smelled of book dust and glue, and he found himself modestly wealthy.

The lawyer clicked shut the catch on his briefcase with satisfaction.

"That concludes all the legal requirements, Mr. Hanford. The balance will be transferred to your account as you specified."

He stood up from the desk and extended his hand. Nick rose from his chair and shook it. His wife, Pamela, remained seated, an expression of suppressed impatience on her thin face. She had come to the reading of the will out of curiosity, but the lawyer had been delayed on his cab drive from the airport, and they had been forced to wait for almost an hour. Pam hated to wait for others.

"I don't know what to think, Mr. Douglas," Nick said. "It's all been so unexpected. I always thought Papa Joe was broke."

Douglas smiled indulgently.

"Some men like to play their cards close to their vest, Mr. Hanford. Have you thought about what you will do with the money?"

"No. I never dreamed I'd have any." He glanced at his wife, but she had her head turned to look out the rain-spotted panes of glass at the grey stone façade across the street. "Look, you're staying in Montreal overnight, right?"

The lawyer nodded.

"Maybe Pam and I can take you out to dinner, to thank you for what you've done."

A wistful look came into the lawyer's corpulent face. He shook his head.

"I'd like that very much, but I have another engagement. Will you excuse me for a moment? Just wait here, the copies of the documents are being printed up and someone will bring them to you shortly."

Douglas hefted his briefcase and left through a side door of the office, closing it softly behind him. Nick sat back down on his chair. At least the padded seat was comfortable. The murmur of traffic in the wet street four stories below came through the narrow crack of an open double-hung window, along with the faint odour of gasoline.

"What are you going to do with the money?" Pam asked, studying her manicured fingernails.

"I don't know yet. I haven't had time to think."

Several minutes passed. A young blonde woman in a brown tweed business suit with a short skirt opened the door of the office from the hallway and looked around. She held a stack of legal-sized file folders on her arm.

"Where is Mr. Douglas?"

Nick pointed to the other door. She nodded and crossed the office to the door, opening it without knocking. It closed silently on its pneumatic closer.

"I think you should invest—" Pamela began to say.

A stifled shriek came from the other room. Nick met his wife's startled gaze and stood up. He took a step toward the door. It opened, and the young woman stumbled through, holding onto the bronze door knob to keep herself on her feet.

"It's Mr. Douglas," she said in a tiny voice.

"Is he sick?" Nick asked.

"He killed himself in the bathroom. There's blood everywhere."

They had to wait for the arrival of the police. They remained seated in the same chairs they had occupied during the reading, while a young lawyer stood at the inner door to make sure nobody entered the scene of the suicide. Pamela declined the offer of her husband's hand. She sat clutching her leather purse on her lap.

"It's another sign," he said quietly.

"What are you talking about?" she demanded in an irritable whisper.

"As the Alignment approaches, chaos will continue to increase. There will be progressively more crimes, more violence, more suicides."

"Nick, get a grip on yourself. You sound like a lunatic."

"I know how it sounds, Pam, but I'm telling you, all the signs are right. Everything fits."

"I'm tired of hearing about your conspiracy theory."

He studied her pale features, a trouble frown on his freckled forehead.

"It's not my theory, it's an ancient prophecy. Why won't you listen?"

She barked derisive laughter that drew the glance of the junior lawyer at the door. He let his gaze wander back to the ceiling.

"Can't you get it through your thick skull, Nick? Nobody ever listened to your crackpot ideas except your grandfather, and now he's dead. Everyone just humours you until you stop talking."

He sat back, his lips compressed into a thin line. His wife was upset and didn't know what she was saying. This wasn't the place to get into an argument with her. After a while, he nodded to himself and smiled. He knew what he was going to do with the money. He would buy a farm.

2.

He quit his job as floor manager with Ogilvy's Department Store in Montreal the next day. His wife did not object. There was no practical reason for him to keep working, and in any case, for the past few months they had found little to say to each other. All marriages cool, but sometimes rigor mortis sets in. Increasingly Pamela had been spending all her free hours at faculty meetings or in the university library researching her book on early French-Canadian poets. The academic climate at McGill was intensely competitive. "Publish or perish" was not a cliché for his wife but an imperative. She was determined to attain tenure, and what she lacked in intellectual brilliance she made up for with sheer tenacity.

She sometimes told him with a trace of contempt in her voice that he should demand a higher management position at Ogilvy's. His response, that he was content with his present job, infuriated her, and they would argue into the night. Similar arguments over equally trivial matters became common, but lately the arguments had stopped. It was not because Pam agreed with his views, but only that she had ceased to care.

While serving out his final weeks of notice training his replacement in the store, he bought an abandoned farm in rural Nova Scotia sight unseen, apart from a handful of photographs e-mailed from the local real estate agent. They showed a modest white two-story clapboard farmhouse set between two mature oak trees, and beyond it a red barn.

It was the barn that sold him on the place. Built into one end was an old-fashioned Dutch windmill. The sheer incongruity of its sloping sides merged into the ass end of the otherwise conventional barn was irresistible. Its enormous canvas-covered sails rose high above the gambrel roof, which admittedly looked a bit sway-backed in the pictures. However, the agent assured Nick by telephone that the structures of both the barn and house were sound.

A farm boy himself, his immaculately barbered hair had never quite lost its sun-bleached look, nor could his starched white shirt collars and silk ties hide the tendency of his neck to redden in the summers. Nick harboured few illusions about the task he was taking on. The fifty-seven-acre property in Nova Scotia had been left abandoned for more than twenty years following the death of its last occupant, an elderly farmer named Elijah Dekker. Until recent years the field had been leased to a neighbouring farmer for growing hay, but the house and barn had not been regularly maintained.

The real estate agent was an Acadian by the name of Earl LeBlanc. His French accent sounded radically different from anything Nick had heard in Montreal. At first Nick tried talking to him in French, but soon gave up when he found the agent's broken English easier to understand over the phone.

"Why wasn't the place sold after the old man died?"

"It the old story, eh? The farm, she go to Dekker's niece when the old man die. She not want to sell, but she not want to live there either, so she leave the place empty. Now she dead, and her daughter in big hurry to sell, sell, sell, so that is why you get so good a price."

"That's kind of strange, isn't it?" Nick said. "I mean, if the niece wasn't going to live there, why wouldn't she sell? Why let it run down and lose value?"

He could almost hear the shrug of the agent.

"It happen all the time. The farm was in the Dekker family for many generations, you know? It have sentimental value and she is not able to bring herself to let it go out of the family. But she is last one, other than her daughter who live in Florida and don't care about the old place."

When he told Pamela about the farm, she said nothing at first, but even before he asked her to come with him to Nova Scotia he saw a preview of her answer in the tightening lines at the corners of her cool grey eyes and the droop of her red mouth.

"You don't need to work any longer, Pam. The money from Papa Joe is enough to keep both of us for the rest of our lives, if we don't go crazy with it. We'll be somewhere safe and self-sufficient when the riots start in the cities. We can put in a garden and raise chickens, maybe a few goats—"

She brushed a strand of long, black hair from her cheek and folded her arms across her flat chest.

"Jesus, Nick, what are you thinking? You're thirty-seven years old. Do you know how much work is involved in restoring an abandoned farm? This place will kill you."

"I'm not planning on restoring it," he said patiently. "I just want to make it liveable. We don't want to be caught in Montreal when the food riots hit. You know it's coming, Pam, I've shown you the signs."

It was the first time she had ever glared at him with naked hatred. It hit him with an almost physical force in the pit of his stomach. He only half attended to the tirade she unleashed.

"Your survivalist theories make me sick. Do you know what you are? You're a conspiracy nut. All that crazy shit about planetary alignments and prophecies and cosmic cycles. All those New Age books you read. I'm not giving up my position at McGill just to humour your whims. In two years I'll have tenure. That's final, Nick. Not another word, I'm through talking about it."

The next day, he left their condominium and took a room at a hotel. She did not try to stop him. It was surprisingly easy to separate himself from her. After eight years of marriage they each owned their own cars. The condo was in both names jointly, and was paid off. There was no dog, no cat, and no children. Neither of them mentioned the word "divorce," but Nick could see it looming in his future, like a thunderhead on the horizon. He stayed in the hotel only long enough to finish his term of notice at Ogilvy's, then packed the trunk of his blue, five-year-old Accord with books, clothes, family photographs, his telescope, and a few keepsakes, and drove east.

3.

The Dekker farm was located just outside the village of South Maitland, about a quarter of a mile from the muddy banks of the Shubenacadie River, not far from where it emptied itself into the Bay of Fundy. It was the heart of what had once been a thriving agricultural region of Nova Scotia. Many of the smaller farms had ceased to produce as their owners aged and died off. Their children retained little enthusiasm for the hard life of working the rich, red soil—not when they could move to the city of Truro less than half an hour away and make a better wage in a warehouse or a lumber yard.

Nick followed the busy 102 south from Truro and took the Shubenacadie turnoff onto a narrow secondary highway that bent its way between low forested hills and rolling pastures. Not all the farms were abandoned. He passed newly planted fields, and meadows from which horses and cows watched his transition with placid indifference. The warm spring air blowing through the open window of the car held a smell of damp manure and newly cut grass that made him feel energized and alert. It awoke memories of his childhood on the family farm that came to him as flashes of imagery.

The Shubenacadie River cut across the green land like an open wound. The river itself was unimpressive, but on either side erosion had exposed broad mud flats the colour of blood. Not far beyond the bridge, the highway took a sharp bend and mounted a steep hill. He nearly missed the unpaved road that led to the farm, and had to hit the brakes when he caught a glimpse of the sign from the corner of his eye. The road bent back sharply from the highway and was at a lower level, so that from the car it was almost invisible. Backing down the highway, which for the moment was empty, he turned onto the gravel.

The old Dekker place occupied a gentle rise at the end of the road. He turned up its long and somewhat intimidating driveway. Note to self, he thought: Before winter comes get a truck with a plough blade. To the left side of the driveway was a wide expanse of what had once been an open hayfield, but was now a field of tall brush and saplings. A narrower band of similar brush on the right side separated the driveway from a woodlot of mature spruce and maple. The red barn was set at an angle some distance behind the house, its doors facing east toward the river, which lay unseen below the crest on the far side of the field.

Earl LeBlanc stood leaning against the fender of his white Ford Explorer. They shook hands. He was almost a foot shorter than Nick's rangy six-two, and the top of his balding head was burnt red by the sun and peeling beneath wisps of blond hair, but his smile was either genuine or a very good imitation.

"Long drive, eh?"

"I didn't expect you to get here before me."

LeBlanc shrugged his shoulders and pursed his lips.

"I am down this way when you call me from Truro, so I decide to just come and wait for you."

He passed Nick a ring with several antique keys on it, and one weathered brass Yale key that Nick assumed must be for the front door of the house. Attached to the ring was a plastic oval with the name of the real estate company.

"Let me show you around the house," LeBlanc said, taking Nick by the arm. "It got some old furniture you might be able to use until you buy better."

Nick held open the aluminum screen door for the agent. It was unfinished aluminum, of the kind that isn't sold any longer. The deadbolt on the inner wooden panel door unlocked easily. Nick paused on the concrete step to look up at a colourful symbol painted on a small circular board above the entrance. The agent stuck his sunburned head out and looked up. He grinned at Nick.

"They call them a hex sign. She for good luck, they say."

"Do you believe in it?"

The agent chuckled.

"No, I don't believe in that foolishness."

The interior was about what Nick had expected. Actually, it was similar to the house in which he had spent his early childhood. An entrance hall, a living room, a parlour, a large kitchen with an old-fashioned wood stove for cooking beside a small electric range, and a walk-in pantry. The floors were plain planks covered in brightly patterned sheets of oilcloth that did not quite reach the walls. The faded and peeling wallpaper was floral. At some point around the mid-1950s the house had received new wiring and plumbing, so it was not quite as primitive as it might have been.

"No power," the agent said, clicking the parlour light switch on and off. "That mean no water either, since the pump in the cellar run on electricity, but you got a hand pump in the kitchen that still work."

"I'll call the power company today and see about getting it turned back on," Nick murmured.

He followed LeBlanc up the steep staircase. The upper floor had one large bedroom, two small rooms, and a full bathroom. The agent sat heavily on the bed in the large room and bounced up and down on the uncovered mattress. A cloud of dust arose in the beam of sunlight that shone through fly-specked panes of the window.

"Good enough for a few night, eh?"

"I guess it will have to do," Nick said. He wondered what might be living in the mattress.

LeBlanc got up and went to a corner of the room, where the oilcloth was curled away from the floor. He stepped on it, but it sprang back up. Grunting to himself, he pulled on the corner and peeled the oilcloth away from the floorboards for several feet. Nick saw some markings in pink chalk underneath.

"Look like some kid been drawing something under here."

Nick studied the lines of chalk with curiosity. A tickle of foreboding made the skin between his shoulders tense. The symbols were familiar, but he could not place them. The agent let the oilcloth snap back into place and Nick shrugged to himself. He had probably seen them in one of his books.

"Your wife, she come down later?" LeBlanc asked.

Nick explained that he would be living alone. To his credit, LeBlanc did not prolong the discomfort.

"That how women is, eh?" he said with a smile that was half apology. "They do the thing in their own good time."

They left the house to look at the barn. Above its double doors was another hex sign, much larger than the one on the house and of a different design. Even though the paint was badly peeled, it was easy to make out its radial pattern. It looked a bit like a snowflake painted in red and green.

Perched on top of the bowed ridge of the barn were two large black birds. Crows, Nick thought, then changed his mind as he got nearer. They were too big for crows. They must be ravens. They were enormous birds. There was something almost unnerving about the way they cocked their long, curved beaks and eyed his approach.

"I wonder where they come from?" he said, pointing at the birds.

"There are farm all around," LeBlanc told him. "The grain, she attract mice. The mice attract birds. These two, I bet you they live here somewhere. They live a long time, you know? Maybe hundred years, maybe even more."

"I think that's just folklore," Nick said gently.

LeBlanc pursed his lips.

"Anyway, it what I was told by my father when I was a boy."

Nick's spirits lifted when he walked around the barn and saw the windmill. It was completely authentic and must have been at least a hundred and fifty years old. The canvas covers on the sails was largely intact, although they were probably rotten after so many years of neglect, he thought.

LeBlanc pulled open one of the double doors at the front of the barn, and they stepped inside. The air was cooler. The sun had not yet had a chance to heat it up. A corner of the barn was occupied by an old wagon. Horseflies buzzed lazily from the shadows of an empty stall. Wagon tracks and the impressions of horses' hooves rutted the dirt floor, all captured years ago like a photograph in the mud as it dried.

Nick's attention was drawn to the rear of the barn, where a great wooden shaft extended from the top of the windmill down to a support bracket and a set of massive iron gears. The shaft was as thick as a telephone pole and appeared to be made of oak. Offset from the base of the shaft was a standing cylinder of black iron some six feet tall and as thick through its middle as a large barrel. Its surface was unbroken except for a single slot near its middle, but it was tied into the shaft by a huge gear at its crown.

For several minutes Nick studied the gears, trying to make sense of them. At last he frowned at LeBlanc.

"It doesn't seem to do anything except turn this iron spindle."

The Acadian shrugged. "I don't know about that."

"Does it work?"

Another shrug.

There was a breeze outside. While the agent waited in silence, Nick spent a couple of minutes studying the guts of the mad contraption, and finally pulled down on a large wooden lever. A thud vibrated the entire structure of the barn. He felt it through the dirt floor beneath his feet. A shower of dust came down from the hayloft. Slowly, the vertical shaft began to rotate. The iron cylinder turned much more slowly, but with shrieks of protest that set Nick's teeth on edge.

"She need some grease," LeBlanc shouted helpfully over the ear-splitting noise.

Nick slammed the lever back up. With another shudder, the shaft stopped. When he turned to the little Acadian, his freckled face beamed with pure delight.

"I love it."

4.

In the morning, Nick drove to Truro to look for a pickup truck. He needed something to haul lumber and other supplies from town to the farm while he worked on the house and barn over the summer, and a more rugged vehicle than the Accord that would handle unploughed roads when the snows came. He could afford to buy new but saw no reason to waste his money.

There were more used car lots in Truro than he would have expected, given the size of the community, but he reminded himself that it was an industrial hub that served as a warehouse and shipping centre for most of the province. It had more the look of a giant industrial park than a place where people lived. There were tractor-trailers everywhere, coming and going on the streets or parked in rows on large asphalt lots beside soulless, flat-roofed buildings made of corrugated steel panels.

"See anything you like?"

Nick glanced across the dirt and gravel lot at the dark-green GMC that had caught his eye as he drove past Pye Chevrolet on Prince Street. It was more than a few years old, with some dings in the side panels, but the steel bracket on the front looked to him like the mount for a plough blade.

"Maybe."

The man in the powder-blue suit and colourful silk tie who had magically appeared as Nick was getting out of the Accord extended his hand with a smile.

"Jim Michaels. Everyone calls me Jimmy."

Nick took his hand reluctantly and said his own name. The salesman had a surprisingly pleasant handshake. His grey-green eyes flickered across at the truck, then back to Nick's face.

"Four-wheel drive, seven years old, low mileage, new tires and battery, no rust."

"She's set up for a plough?"

The smile broadened.

"That she is, sir. Great way to make some extra money in the winter. She'll practically pay for herself."

Nick hesitated for barely half a second.

"Maybe I can take it for a test dive?"

"You sure can." The salesman took him by the arm and guided him around a water-filled puddle toward the truck. "Mind the potholes, we're in the middle of getting repaved. You look her over, sit in her, while I get the keys. I'll be right back."

The salesman did not even ask to see his license, just passed him the keys and told him to bring them to the office when he got back. I must have a trustworthy face, Nick thought as he climbed into the cab and started the engine. Or maybe it was just how they did things Down East. It had been more than ten years since he had driven a truck, or a manual transmission for that matter, but old habits come back fast. The truck pulled forward easily and lurched on its stiff suspension through the potholes.

He started to pull out of the lot and onto the street. A horn blasted in his ear through the open window, and he hit the brake. The truck stalled. He'd forgotten the clutch.

"Asshole! Learn to drive!"

A black SUV shot past and cut into the entrance of the dealership, missing the right front fender of the pickup by inches. The driver was a thin teenager with a goatee and a tattoo of a skull on the side of his neck. He gave Nick the finger as he went by.

Nick clenched the steering wheel and exhaled slowly. What was wrong with people today? They were driving crazy, cutting each other off, blasting their horns for nothing. On the way into the city he had seen a speeding car lose control and go into the ditch. There were always one or two people on the roads who couldn't drive, but today it seemed like half the drivers were trying to kill the other half. Could it be the coming Alignment? He had read speculations that as the alignment of the planets predicted by the ancient Sumerian prophecy neared perfection, it would cast ripples across the Earth that would affect the way people acted, but nobody could predict how its influence would show itself. He felt normal enough. Maybe it was just a coincidence.

He saw the blue suit hurrying up behind him at a quick walk.

"You all right, sir?"

"Fine. I stalled the engine. Just gave me a surprise, that's all."

The salesman shook his head and frowned as he looked around the corner of the showroom where the SUV had vanished.

"Those young people drive like maniacs. Got to watch them all the time. Sixteen's too young to drive. I've got a son, but I won't let him get his license until he's eighteen."

The kid in the SUV had looked at least nineteen to Nick, but he didn't say anything.

He took the truck around a few blocks, then did a short loop on the highway to see how it handled at speed. By the time he brought it back, his mind was made up. It was what he needed.

There was no one at the front desk of the office. He laid the keys on the desk in a bin labelled "keys" and wandered into the glass-walled showroom. It looked deserted. Quiet music played in the background. He heard an angry voice from somewhere toward the rear and rounded the corner, then stopped dead. Half a dozen men and two women were gathered in a loose circle around the punk in the black leather jacket who had cut him off earlier. The punk was waving his arms and yelling. Nick couldn't make out what he was saying—his voice was high-pitched with fury and almost inarticulate. Only a few words made it through.

"Cheat me . . . bunch of crooks . . . everyone needs to know . . . I'm not finished . . . don't lay your hand on me . . ."

The salesman in the blue suit held up his hands and waved them in a placating gesture while he made soothing sounds, but the wiry teenager was not listening. Abruptly, he snatched up a chromed, steel-frame chair and threw it at a plate glass window. One corner of the chair hit the glass and cracked it. The young man was almost frothing at the mouth. His lips writhed away from his teeth and his black, close-set eyes had a crazy wildness. He pushed past a middle-aged woman in a white blouse and black skirt, nearly knocking her down, and stalked out of the showroom.

The salesman told another man in a tweed suit to call the police. He turned and saw Nick. There was blood trickling from his left nostril and his nose had begun to swell and turn purple on one side.

"Hell of a day," he said, forcing a smile.

"I'll buy the truck," Nick told him. "On condition that you have it driven out to my farm."

"What, no haggling on the price?"

"I'm sure it's fair."

The salesman put his arm around Nick's shoulder in a fatherly way.

"You're my kind of customer. Let's go to the office and I'll draw up the papers."

5.

Over the weeks that followed, Nick spent every minute of daylight working on the house and the barn. He used the old GMC pickup to haul the supplies he needed from Truro. When the autumn came on, he told himself, he would buy a second-hand plough blade for it so that he could clear his driveway of winter snow. In the meantime, there were plenty of other uses for the pickup.

The electricity had been easy enough to get turned on, but the plumbing proved to be more problematical. The rusting two-cylinder piston water pump in the damp cellar was an antique that hadn't turned in twenty years. He thought about replacing it with a new jet pump, then decided to try to fix it. For days he struggled with it as old and almost forgotten farm skills returned to his hands. When at last the big flywheel began to revolve on its own, there was no one there to congratulate him, so he just nodded his head with silent satisfaction.

Years spent standing around inside a department store wearing a suit and tie had left him soft. Working shirtless under the bright spring sun, his freckled skin burned, and then tanned, making his blue eyes stand forth in strikingly contrast above his high cheekbones. As his skin darkened, his sandy hair grew lighter, until it was the same straw colour of his youth. His Norwegian heritage on his mother's side became more evident.

The first day that he split firewood with the rusty double-bladed axe he found in the barn, the blisters on his hands bled. The second day he wore leather work gloves, and by the fifth day the pain went away. He used the wood for cooking in the kitchen stove. The electric range worked, but he liked cooking with wood. He rented a brush cutter and worked it back and forth across his field until nothing stood higher than its reciprocating blades. Open fires were not illegal. He burned the brush and weeds as he cut them.

It was when he was using a rented roto-tiller to till up a small patch of soil for a vegetable garden that he found the chain. The front-mounted blade of the tiller bucked and stalled. Nick assumed he had hit a rock. Setting the machine aside, he dug around with a pick and shovel where the blade had struck. The chain lay less than a foot beneath the surface of the sod. He uncovered it as best he could with the shovel, then squatted and brushed away the damp red soil with his fingers.

It was made of black iron and massive, each link more than four inches long and as thick as his thumb. He looked closer, then spat on one of the links and rubbed it with his finger. His eyes widened. Each link was slightly different, which meant that the chain was hand-forged, which meant that it must be old. Obviously it was a ship's anchor chain, but what was it doing buried in his field? He wondered if it would be of any interest to a local museum as he continued to dig to expose its ends so that he could drag it out of his garden plot.

"What's that you got there?"

Nick turned and squinted into the sun. He shielded his eyes with his muddy forearm and saw the stocky outline of a man. Blinking away sunspots, he stepped out of the garden plot and to the side.

"You walk quiet. I didn't even hear you coming."

The other was around sixty years old, with straight grey hair that hung over his ears and a curling grey beard with a streak of white down its centre. He wore a long-brimmed hunter-orange cap, a red-and-white chequered shirt with the sleeves rolled up, and blue denim bib-dungarees that hung on straps from his broad shoulders. His wide-set hazel eyes had a liveliness that seemed foreign to the slackness of his face. He extended his hand.

"Name's Hans Hoffmann. My farm's on the other side of that windbreak over there, down toward the river. Heard you working the past couple weeks and decided to come and say hello."

Nick brushed off his palm and shook the older man's hand. His blunt fingers were surprisingly powerful. There was black dirt under his nails.

"You've got a good, firm handshake, Mr. Hoffmann."

"Hans. We're neighbours now."

"Are you the person who used to cut the field after Dekker died?" Nick asked with sudden inspiration.

Hoffmann nodded.

"Did it for eleven years, but got to the point where I wasn't making any money from the hay, so I had to stop. Hated to see this field get overgrown, though."

"Well, it's clear now," Nick said.

Hoffmann kicked the stump of a sapling that Nick had cut off near the root with the brush cutter. There were similar stumps scattered all across the field.

"I'm not planning on planting the field, so it's clear enough for me," Nick explained.

Both fell silent and stood looking into the hole at the black chain.

"How do you suppose it got there?" Nick asked.

Hoffmann took his sweat-stained cap off and scratched the scalp under his matted grey hair with a thumbnail.

"Likely buried just to get rid of it. Before my time. I never knew it was here."

"You'd think if someone was going to bury it just to get rid of it, they'd coil it up."

"That makes sense," Hoffmann agreed.

His dancing hazel eyes followed the direction in which the length of the chain pointed. On the crest of the rise at the far end of the field grew a clump of stunted alders. Nick noticed where the older man was looking.

"There's a pool fed by some kind of artesian spring in those trees," he said.

"Yup, I know there is. Water's no good, though."

"Too bad. It would be useful for watering livestock."

"Dekker tried it for irrigation, but it wilted his crops, so he only used it that single season. Bad year for him, that was."

There was the awkward silence of two men who knew nothing about each other.

"Will you come into the house for some coffee?" Nick asked.

Hoffmann smiled.

"Since you're offering, I won't say no."

"I've got white rum, too. Would you like a drink?"

"Coffee's fine."

They walked back toward the house together. Nick gestured at the windmill.

"What do you suppose would possess a man to build something like that?"

"Don't know. They call it Dekker's Folly. Not referring to Josiah Dekker, mind you. It was built long before he was born."

"How old is it?"

Hoffmann shook his head.

"Nobody around here knows. More than a century, that's certain. Maybe two hundred years."

"Really? You think it's that old?" Nick was delighted.

"Maybe. Nobody knows. It was always here, as long as anyone can remember."

Hoffmann noticed the stubby reflector telescope set up on its equatorial mounting at the corner of the house. The end of the short tube was capped to keep out the sun and the bugs.

"You one of those star-gazers?"

Nick shrugged. "It's a hobby. I like following the planets. I'm mainly interested in astrology."

Hoffmann clapped him on the shoulder in a companionable way and peered into Nick's face with his disturbingly expressive eyes.

"You're a bright young feller. I knew it the minute I saw you."

In the kitchen, Nick filled the electric kettle with water for instant coffee. While it boiled, he washed his hands and arms in the kitchen sink, dried them, and pulled on a white T-shirt that hung over the back of a chair. Hoffmann sat at the table and waited with his hands folded, his head turning this way and that as though he searched for something.

"Dekker was a bright feller, too. He used to read all the time. You find any of his books?"

"Didn't find anything like that," Nick said, bringing two steaming mugs to the kitchen table.

They sipped the brew and talked about the local people of South Maitland. After a while, Hoffmann stood to leave.

"Tell you what I'll do. I'll get my tractor and we'll see if the two of us can pull that chain out of the ground. How about that?"

"Sounds like a plan," Nick told him.

6.

In mid-afternoon Hoffmann drove up the driveway on a bright red Massy-Ferguson tractor that looked almost brand-new. He turned off the gravel and across the field to the garden plot, where he sat with the engine idling. Nick set aside the axe he had been using to split firewood and walked over.

"Told you I'd be back," Hoffmann said, spitting to the side from his seat.

"You're a man of your word."

"I do what I say I'll do."

He reached behind his seat and took out a coil of heavy yellow nylon rope, then threw it down to Nick.

"Tie this onto a link of that black chain, and we try some horse-power."

Nick hefted the heavy rope.

"I'm not much good with knots. Maybe you should tie it on, so that it won't come loose."

Hoffmann barked a short laugh.

"It's your chain, son. Why should I get my hands dirty?"

Your hands are already dirty, Nick thought. But he just nodded and bent to tie the end of the rope through a link of the chain. He used a square knot, hoping it would not slip. Nylon rope tended to stretch under tension. There was a massive bracket for towing on the back of the tractor. He looped the rope around it and tied it tight.

The bearded farmer revved the engine on the tractor and slowly let out the clutch. As Nick had anticipated, the rope began to stretch. He saw that the end of the rope where it was tied to the chain was about to slip through the knot and hollered at Hoffmann to stop pulling. Hoffmann turned in his seat to scowl and backed the tractor to slacken the rope. This time, Nick used three knots. The rope did not slip. It pulled tight and got thin, then snapped like a rubber band. The chain was shifted to the side by a few inches.

"It's no good," Nick shouted over the clatter of the tractor's engine. "The rope's not strong enough."

"Untie it. We'll use the tow chain."

The tow chain was of high-quality steel and had welded links. Hoffmann got down from his seat and dragged it from its storage box onto the grass, then handed one end to Nick. There was a heavy bolt with a nut on it through the last link. Nick slid it around the iron chain to make a loop and used the bolt to join it, while the farmer hooked the other end to the tractor.

"This won't break," he told Nick with a wink.

"Maybe it will break the old chain. It must be half rotten after sitting in the ground for so many years."

Hoffmann shook his shaggy head.

"Black iron's strong. It won't rust except just on the surface. Sometimes not even there. Did you know they've got a pillar of black iron in India that has been standing in the wind and rain for sixteen hundred years, and there's no trace of rust on it?"

"I think I read something about that," Nick said. "Nobody knows for sure how the pillar was forged or what was mixed with the iron to keep it from rusting."

"Never underestimate black iron," Hoffmann said in a quiet voice, narrowing his eyes at the chain in its bed of red earth as though it were a sleeping serpent.

He climbed back onto the tractor and Nick stood well to one side. The big rear wheels of the tractor spun in the sod and dug it up, throwing dirt and stones for twenty yards. The front end lifted off the ground and wandered back and forth, like the raised nose of a moose that sniffs the air. The tow chain did not break, but neither did the iron chain move.

"It's no good," Hoffmann said in disgust after he shut the overheating tractor off.

"There must be a lot more of it under the ground," Nick said. "I'll have to dig it out by hand. Or maybe rent a backhoe."

He unhooked the tow chain and coiled it behind the tractor.

Hoffmann spat. He looked frustrated, and more than that, he looked angry, although his anger was well-controlled.

"My advice to you is just leave it where it is. What harm is it doing? Move the garden, leave the chain where it is. Bury it and forget about it."

Nick was bemused by his sudden change of temper, but put it down to country pride. Farmers didn't like to get beaten by a stump or a rock. Or an old piece of chain.

He knew Hoffmann had given him good advice, but he could not take it. The chain fascinated him. He wondered how long it was and how it had gotten there. He wondered if there might be an anchor attached to its end.

"Come into the house. Maybe this time I can get you to drink something stronger than coffee."

"I won't say no."

They went to the front door because it was closer. Hoffmann paused on the slab of concrete that served as a step and stood gazing up at the hex sign. Nick stopped beside him and folded his arms across his T-shirt, studying the wooden disk. Now that he looked at it, the abstract design reminded him of a single staring eye.

"They say it's for good luck."

"Some say that," Hoffmann agreed. "That's not what I was taught."

"What were you taught?" Nick asked curiously.

"Superstitious folk teach that it wards off devils, as long as you don't invite them across the threshold." He grinned. "I'm not superstitious myself."

He held the screen door open for Nick to pass.

In the kitchen, Nick poured Bacardi rum into two glasses and added ice from the antique fridge, which by some miracle worked perfectly. They sat at opposite ends of the table, sipping the cold drinks.

"Are you a widower?" Hoffmann asked.

"No. What makes you ask that?"

Hoffmann pointed a thick index finger at Nick's left hand. Nick realized he was pointing at his wedding band. He had worn it for so long, he tended to forget it was even there.

"My wife is in Montreal."

"When is she coming to join you?"

When indeed, Nick thought. Privately, he doubted Pam would ever give up her career for farm life, not voluntarily at any rate. At least if things got too bad in the city, she would have a refuge. That was about all he could offer her, a place of safety should she need it.

"She's a teacher at McGill University. She has contractual obligations." It sounded weak even in his own ears.

Hoffmann's keen hazel eyes studied him. He nodded toward Nick's wedding ring.

"She had a prior contractual obligation, son. You ought to remind her of that."

"You don't know Pamela," Nick said with a shake of his head.

"I know women. Don't look so surprised. Just because I live on a farm doesn't mean I haven't sowed my share of wild oats."

The image of the shaggy-headed farmer sowing oats struck Nick as both bizarre and a bit repellent. He hid his reaction by taking another drink, then topped off his glass from the bottle. The rum exerted its warming magic on his interior. To his surprise, he found himself talking about his wife.

"We met while she was a graduate student working on her doctoral thesis. You know what a thesis is, don't you?"

Hoffmann raised his bushy eyebrows.

"I'm a farmer, not a moron."

"We really fell for each other hard. There was a chemistry between us. I was out of work then, so I had a lot of free time. She was an activist with Greenpeace and she got me to sign up." Nick smiled apologetically. "Save the seals. Save the whales. I only joined to be close to her."

"Not the crusading type?"

"No, not really. We got married quickly. Maybe too fast, but you can't stop a relationship like what we had between us. For a few years everything went great. Then she started telling me I should look for a more important job, that I was wasting my talent working in a department store. I told her I was satisfied with my job, but she wouldn't accept that. Pam has a lot of personal drive and ambition. I guess I disappointed her."

He lifted his glass and saw Hoffmann studying him with narrowed eyes. The farmer smiled and spread his hands.

"Every marriage weathers a few storms."

"Not like this one," Nick murmured half to himself. "I think it's going to sink the ship."

"Which one is that?"

Nick eyed him defiantly. He saw that Hoffman's glass was nearly empty and refilled it from the bottle.

"What do you know about the Sumerian Alignment?"

"Not a damn thing."

"That's what most people say. It's a prophecy about the end of the world. I got interested in it a few years ago and started to read up on it. In 1953 the Danish archaeologist Thorkild Jacobsen found the ruins of a temple nine miles south of the ancient Sumerian city of Legash. Buried beneath the ruins in a dry well were sets of clay cylinders carefully preserved in stone jars. The cylinder texts told of the coming of a great cosmic alignment that would open the gate of the afterworld and bring destruction and chaos over the entire Earth. They even specified the date."

"Don't keep me in suspense," Hoffmann said with a grin. "When it is?"

"A week from today."

"That's not much time." The farmer sipped his rum. "How did your wife handle the news?"

"At first Pam laughed about my hobby, as she called it, but when she saw that I was getting serious, she turned angry. She tried to get me to drop the whole thing, but it's not something you can just set aside." Nick waved his glass for emphasis. "Not when you realize that it is really going to happen."

"What did you do?"

"I tried to warn people about what is coming, but most of our friends just laughed it off. Pam said I was embarrassing her every time I opened my mouth. I don't know, I guess I was at that. But what could I do? I couldn't just let people die without at least trying to warn them, could I?"

"Why not? You're not your brother's keeper. Take my advice, you do the smart thing and just worry about yourself."

Nick drained his glass and shook his head.

"That's a cynical way to look at it."

Hoffmann laughed.

"I wouldn't judge you, son. It's what any sensible person would do. Save-the-world crusader types are a pain in the ass."

He watched from his front step as Hoffman drove his tractor down the driveway without a backward look. The words of the grizzled old farmer still echoed in his mind. Maybe I am a pain in the ass, Nick thought, but I have to be honest about what I know is coming, even if nobody wants to hear it.

7.

That evening, after washing up the dinner dishes, he called his wife on the cellphone. It rang for a long time before she picked up. The landline in their condo had caller recognition. Pam had insisted on it to prevent her students from pestering her at home. He could almost see her in his mind, standing beside the phone with her arms crossed, wondering whether to answer.

"Hello, Nick."

"Hello, Pam." He hesitated. "I've been listening to the news about the riots on the radio and wanted to make sure you are all right."

"I'm fine. The news media is blowing everything out of proportion. I've only seen one riot, and that was students at the university library. It was nothing. The police were called and a few kids got pepper-sprayed."

"The CBC News reports says they've been breaking out all over the city. And it isn't just Montreal. It's happening in New York, Los Angeles, Toronto, London, Paris, Tokyo. All around the world."

"It's an hysterical reaction to this Sumerian Prophecy nonsense. People have heard so much about it on the Internet, they are getting frightened. But it's only the noodles, not those with any common sense."

"There are an awful lot of people who believe in the prophecy, Pam. More every day, from what is being said on the radio."

She laughed.

"It's all highly entertaining. I was in the faculty lounge, and Norm Lamond was talking about it. You should have heard him imitate that prophecy person, what's-his-name?"

Nick thought for a second.

"Do you mean Peter Simmons?"

"That's him! The one you like. Norm got his accent down perfectly. It was hysterical, Nick. Everyone laughed so hard, they were almost rolling on the floor."

"That would be something to see," he said dryly.

"Oh, don't be so serious. The whole thing is completely ridiculous. After the fatal date passes, there are a lot of people who are going to look foolish."

"You mean like me?"

"No, not like you. I'm talking about the crazy people. You were never crazy about this prophecy foolishness—not insane crazy, I mean. Still, I bet you're going to blush when you come back to Montreal after all this nonsense blows over."

He pulled out a wooden chair and sat down at the kitchen table, resting the elbow of his phone arm on its surface.

"Pam, I'm not coming back."

She laughed again, but this time it sounded brittle.

"Of course you're coming home, Nick. We both know this is only a little vacation for you, just a way to celebrate your inheritance. I understand. It's good for us to have some time apart. We were getting stale. When you come home we can examine your employment situation more rationally. We'll work something out."

"Didn't you hear me?"

"Hear what?"

"I'm not coming back to Montreal, Pam. Not now, not after the Alignment, not ever."

There was silence at the other end.

"We'll talk about it later, Nick. You're still caught up in this ancient prophecy nonsense. Once the date of the Alignment passes, you'll feel differently."

He bit his lower lip and frowned. There was no point in arguing with her. He recognized her mood. She would not listen. Still, he had to try to warn her.

"Just do something for me, will you, Pam?"

"Maybe. What do you want me to do?"

"Don't go out at night. Stay away from crowds. If you do have to go out, don't go alone."

She sighed so forcefully, he heard it.

"Nick—"

"Just do what I say," he said, more harshly than he intended. "Why can't you ever just do what I tell you to do?"

There were several seconds of silence.

"Well, if that's your attitude, I can see there's no sense talking to you."

"Pam, I didn't mean to bark."

"Goodbye, Nick. I'll talk to you again after the Alignment, when you're back to being your normal self."

"I am my normal self," he protested. But she was already gone.

It was always the same when they had an argument. He could never win. Sometimes he wondered why he even bothered to say anything.

He sat at the table for several minutes, staring at the half-empty bottle of white rum on the cupboard shelf. Whispering a curse, he opened his phone and accessed its directory, then dialled a long-distance number. A woman with a Texas accent answered.

"I'm trying to reach Peter Simmons."

There was a pause.

"Who is calling?"

"This is Nick Hanford."

"How is it that you know my husband?"

Her voice sounded strained. A coldness began to spread inside him.

"We met over the Internet. I'm doing research on the Sumerian Prophecy and your husband was kind enough to help me find some of my source materials."

"Pete is dead," she said in a leaden voice.

"What? I was just talking to him a few weeks ago."

"Last night. Someone shot him in the back of the head while he was getting into his car in our driveway."

"That's terrible," Nick said. He struggled to find words. An image of Peter's cheerful face came into his mind. It was the image in the photograph on the back cover of his last book.

"Yes, it is terrible. I'm sorry, Mr. Hanford, I can't talk to you now."

"No, of course not, I understand. Did the police catch the person who shot him?"

"No. There were no witnesses."

"I'm terribly sorry," he said.

There was no one on the phone. He looked at it for a few moments, feeling tired and a bit lost, then turned it off.

8.

It was the following morning, while he washed off a section of the chain with a bucket of water to photograph it close up with the hope that he could have it identified at the marine museum in Halifax, that he noticed the hieroglyphs. He called them that in his own mind because he did not know what else to call them. They were angular symbols impressed into each link, one symbol per link. He counted the different shapes and discovered that there were twenty-four unique symbols, and that they repeated in various multiples and sequences along the length of the chain like some kind of arcane code.

After taking the pictures, he got a notepad and pencil from the house and drew out the symbols. For a time he sat on his front step, studying them. They resembled the letters of a strange alphabet, yet looked oddly familiar. He had the sense that he had seen them before but could not remember where, until he was putting the notepad away in a drawer in the kitchen. He snatched it back and ran up the stairs to the large bedroom. Tossing it on the bed, he grabbed the curled corner of the oilcloth in both hands and peeled it completely away from the floorboards.

Beneath the oilcloth, drawn in coloured chalks that had become smudged and dim over the years, was a large double-circle with more of the strange symbols written between its bands. In the centre of the circle was drawn a complex seal of some sort. As he studied its uncouth angles, a shadow passed over the window and across the circle on the floor. It was gone before he could turn his head. He heard a series of harsh croaks that diminished in the distance. One of the ravens had flown past, casting the shadow of its large black wings into the bedroom.

Nick spent the next twenty minutes drawing the circle and copying the symbols on the floor into the notebook, then sat on the bed and compared the hieroglyphs around the circle with those on the chain. The shapes were identical. Old Dekker had been more than just a bright feller who liked to read. Nick had learned enough during his studies of astrology and ancient prophecy to know that this was a ritual circle of some kind. That fitted with the hex sign over the door and the one on the barn. What did the German immigrants call those who practiced magic? Hexmeisters? No, hexenmeisters. That was it. Old Dekker must have been a hexenmeister. He remembered reading that the power to hex was hereditary. Maybe the whole Dekker clan had been into the black arts.

A knock on the front door made him jump. He went downstairs and opened the door to Earl LeBlanc. The balding real estate agent brought his winning grin into the living room. He carried a padded mailing envelope in his hand with something bulky inside that pushed out its sides.

"You done a lot of work on the house," he said with appreciation, looking around.

"It's a start," Nick said. "Would you like some coffee?"

"No, I can't stay, I just come to drop this package off for you. I think maybe you would be interested in it more than me."

Nick took the mailer and saw that its end had been opened. He peeked inside. It contained a wad of papers and a book of some kind. The upper-left corner of the mailer bore the name Judeth Marino and a Florida address.

"What is it?"

LeBlanc shrugged and wiped the sweat from his crown with his palm, then transferred it to his pants at the side of his thigh.

"You remember when I tell you about the daughter of the niece who own this house and sell it?"

Nick nodded.

"She send me this. She say the new owner of the house might want it because it part of the history of the house, and she don't want it no more."

Nick carried the padded envelope to a table against the wall and emptied its contents. The papers were covered with writing, symbols, and drawings. What he had assumed to be a book was actually a kind of journal bound in soft brown leather. He leafed through it. The writing was in English in a firm, clear hand, done with a fountain pen in black ink. He turned to the first page. Inscribed in the middle were the words "Thaddeus Dekker, his Book, 1903."

"I try to reach you by phone to see if you want these paper, but you never answer."

"Sorry," Nick said. "I work outside most of the day and leave the cellphone in the house. I don't want it to get ruined by sweat in the pocket of my jeans."

"No matter," LeBlanc told him in his lilting Acadian accent. "I have to be down this way today, so I bring the paper along with me."

"I appreciate it. This looks fascinating."

"So, how you like the house?"

"I like it. The pump's fixed and the water's good. I don't get cable television or the Internet out here, but I don't miss them. I listen to the radio instead. There's a good station in Truro that does local reports."

"You hear about those riots in Los Angeles and Chicago and all those other places? Even in Montreal, I think."

Nick frowned and nodded.

"Things are coming to a head. There's going to be a general breakdown of law and order before the Alignment. I'm just glad to be out of the city."

"What about your wife? How she doing?"

"I talked to her last night. She doesn't want to leave Montreal. She thinks the unrest will blow over."

"I sure hope she right," LeBlanc said, eyeing him keenly. "What I see on the television, it keep getting worse. Everybody going crazy, I think."

Nick nodded. LeBlanc turned to the door.

"Before you go, I want to show you something."

He took the agent outside to the rectangle of turned soil that was supposed to have been his vegetable garden and pointed at the chain.

"Did anyone ever say anything to you about this?"

The little Acadian walked around the rectangle and studied the chain.

"No one say anything to me. It was buried in the ground before you dig it up, right?"

Nick nodded.

"Maybe no one know it was there. It look pretty damn old."

"Do you think the daughter of Dekker's niece would know anything about it?"

LeBlanc shrugged.

"Can you give me her telephone number? I may want to ask her about it."

"Sure, why not?"

Nick walked LeBlanc back to his Explorer and waited while the little Acadian consulted his address book and wrote down the phone number on the back of one of his business cards.

9.

He spent the rest of the morning and the afternoon digging along the path of the chain toward the clump of alders that marked the location of the bitter spring. He wanted to read the notebook and study the papers but would not give up daylight hours to do so. The papers would still be there when he returned to the house at sunset, he told himself.

Nowhere was the chain more than eight or ten inches below the surface of the rough sod, which had been overgrown with saplings and bushes before he cleared it. The roots of the young trees posed a few problems but none he could not solve with his axe. The chain was black as coal and, when cleaned of the damp red earth that clung to it, shone with a kind of dark lustre in the sunlight. He remembered what Hoffmann had said about the enduring properties of old iron, how it could lie in the ground for centuries without rusting. It formed a coating that sealed out the corrosive oxygen in the air, preventing rust from gaining a foothold on the metal.

The wild fancy came into his mind to wonder if the chain had ever been buried at all. If it lay upon the surface of the ground long enough, it was possible that the soil might have accumulated around and over it with the passage of years. But for it to be as deep as it was would require centuries—probably longer than Nova Scotia had been settled by Europeans. Was it possible that the chain had been there before the house was built? An even stranger idea crossed his mind. Was it possible that the barn had been built where it was because of the chain? The back end of the trench he had dug seemed to point directly toward the doors of the barn.

A shadow fell across the chain as he worked to cut away the tough roots that had grown through its links. He straightened his back and looked into a round face surrounded by a halo of white curls. It reminded Nick of the face of a middle-aged cherub. It was tanned but unlined, as though strong emotion seldom passed across it. The eyes were so pale a grey that they were almost white.

The little man, who was pot-bellied and around fifty years of age, was dressed in worn jeans and a ragged denim shirt. He looked like a homeless person, but he smiled in such a guileless way that Nick found himself smiling back. He handed Nick a creased and dirty piece of brown wrapping paper.

Printed in pencil were the words, "This is Charlie Pye. He don't talk but he is a real good worker." There was no signature.

Pye. The name was familiar.

"Are you related to the man who owns the Chevy dealership in Truro?"

A shake of the head sent the round-faced little man's curls dancing.

"Are you looking for work?" Nick asked him. The little man smiled more broadly and nodded.

Nick thought for a few moments. He had not intended to hire a workman, but having an extra set of hands would enable him to complete his survival preparations in time for the Sumerian Alignment. Beyond that, he wanted to lay in firewood for the fall and winter, and had to get it cut soon so that it would at least start to dry. He wanted to get both the house and barn painted, and all the windows reglazed. The windows were six-over-six double-hungs, and the old putty around the edges of the panes of glass had shrunk and dropped out over the years, so that many of the panes were held in place by no more than a few glazier's points. Most of all, he wanted to get the chain exposed. It was an irrational desire, but no less intense for that.

"I couldn't pay much. Have you got a place to sleep?"

Pye shook his head.

"Would you mind sleeping in the loft of the barn?"

Pye shook his head again.

"I can get you a bunk and some blankets. And a kerosene lantern and kerosene stove for making tea and coffee."

He did not want a stranger sleeping in the house with him, but could not think how to say this to the mute labourer without hurting his feelings. Pye seemed to sense what he was thinking and nodded to show that it was fine with him if he slept in the barn.

They carried a cot and mattress from one of the little rooms of the house to the hayloft, which had been unused for twenty years by the look of the dust that had accumulated on its floor. The narrow steel bed frame was light enough to pass up the ladder, followed by the mattress and some bedding. Nick found a soot-stained kerosene lantern. Heating the loft would not be a concern for months, as the nights were getting warmer. If they survived the Alignment, and if Pye was still here in the fall, he would think about what to do for a heat source. He promised Pye that he would buy him a small kerosene cooking stove on his next trip to Truro. The round-faced little mute beamed with happiness.

They returned to the trench. Pye set to work enthusiastically with a pick, loosening the roots and soil around the chain.

Nick left him to it and walked up the gentle slope of the field to the grove of trees on its crest. He pushed his way through the dense alders. These grew in clusters of thin trunks no more than ten feet high, forming a thicket that was interlaced so closely that it took determined force to fit his body between them. The band of alders around the spring was no more than a dozen feet deep. Beyond it he found himself in an open area that was an almost perfect circle. It was a pool of black water perhaps twenty feet across, lined at its margin with large boulders. Bubbles rose at its centre and spread slowly over its inky surface. The overflow from the spring welling up unseen in the depths of the pool found its way out along a narrow but deep gully of stones and gravel that meandered down the far side of the rise toward the river.

The place was unlike anything Nick had ever experienced. All sight of the house, even most of the sounds of Pye's digging, was cut off by the alders. The circle felt ancient, even primordial. He found himself shivering in the shade of the inward-leaning trees and stepped forward into the sunlight. Somehow he knew that the black spring had not changed for centuries, or even thousands of years. The soil must be poor not to support larger trees, he thought—or maybe years ago Dekker had cut them all down, and the alders had grown up in their place.

He leaned over the large, moss-covered rocks at the edge of the pond and tried to peer into its depths. The water was the colour of molasses. He could see the rising strings of tiny bubbles for only two or three feet. He had a sense that it was much deeper, as was often the case with springs. Reaching his hand in, he cupped it and drew up some of the water. It did not look black against his palm. He sipped it, but immediately spat it out. It had a bitter taste laced with the tang of iron. Whatever its source, it was not the same as that of the dug well that fed the house. Maybe that was why the house had been built so far away from the spring—to find well water fit for drinking and for watering livestock.

With greater care, he searched around the near side of the pond, pushing aside weeds and grass that sprouted up between the stones and turning over the thick carpet of soft, green moss with the heel of his boot. He was about ready to give up when he came across the dull sheen of black iron. It was not part of the chain, as he expected, but a kind of angled and rounded iron pipe that led between two large stones and into the black water.

Nick lay down with his chest pressed against pipe. It was about six inches in diameter and as cold as ice through the thin material of his T-shirt. With some reluctance, he reached his arm into the water and felt along the pipe where it disappeared into the depths. At the extreme limit of his reach, he found the rough edge that marked its end. With a grunt, he shifted his shoulders and twisted to reach deeper. His shoulder passed into the water to his armpit. He reached into the pipe and was able to feel the links of the chain, which, as he had suspected, passed through the elbow of the pipe and descended into the spring. The pipe acted as a kind of guide for the chain over the rocks at the rim of the pond.

Something brushed the back of his submerged hand. He let out an involuntary shout and jerked his arm from the water. He studied his fingers anxiously, but they were merely wet. Laughing weakly, he rolled onto his back on the moss that covered the rounded rocks. Some kind of fish had brushed his hand, or maybe a frog. He closed his eyes to enjoy the warm spring sun on his face.

A loud croak made him open them. Perched on one of the alders, a raven stared down at him, then cocked its head to the side as it opened its beak to taste the air. It was near enough that he had a good look at it. The bird's feathers were ragged around the edges. It did not look like a young bird. One of its eyes was milky white, covered with a kind of cataract, which explained the odd angle of its head. He met its black gaze and held it for a dozen seconds. Had he been standing up, the bird would have been near enough to touch.

"Quoth the raven, 'Nevermore,'" he murmured with a smile.

The bird closed its beak and launched itself into the air. He sat up and turned to look after it, but it was nowhere to be seen. Through the alders he heard the angry babble of a voice. It took him more than a minute to force his way back out of the thicket of stubborn trees. He saw Hoffmann standing over Pye, who lay sprawled on his back on the ground. The farmer's fist was clenched and Pye's mouth was bloody. Hoffmann picked up the pick and started to raise it.

"Hey, what's going on?" Nick shouted.

Hoffmann turned to glare at him. His shoulders relaxed and he straightened his back, tossing the pick aside.

"I found this tramp on your land and tried to drive him off, but he won't go."

"I hired him," Nick said, not trying to disguise his irritation. "He works for me."

"What? You hired this good-for-nothing? Everyone around here knows he's not right in the head. You should have asked me first, I would have told you."

"Who I hire is my own business, Mr. Hoffmann."

The farmer's animated hazel eyes danced as he studied Nick's expression and posture.

"Yes, I suppose it is." He smiled sourly. "My mistake."

He extended his hand to Charlie Pye, but the pot-bellied little man cringed away from him and scrambled to his feet on his own. He rubbed the blood from his mouth. Nick saw that his lower lip was split and swollen.

"Still working on this chain, I see," Hoffmann said.

"That's right."

"Didn't take my advice."

"I want to see where it ends."

Hoffmann nodded, staring down at the chain. He seemed to become lost in his own thoughts for several seconds. He looked up, his face expressionless.

"Sorry for the trouble. Just a misunderstanding."

"Don't apologize to me, apologize to Charlie."

Hoffmann glanced at Pye. They stood eyeing each other. At last the farmer turned to go.

"Just stopped by to say hello, and ask if I could help out. I see you don't need my help anymore."

"That's right," Nick agreed.

"I'll go now."

Nick watched until Hoffmann had disappeared into the windbreak of spruce trees that separate his field from that of his neighbour. He approached Pye, who smiled at him ruefully, then winced when his stretched lower lip began to bleed once more.

"Do you want me to take you to the hospital?"

Pye picked up the shovel and pointed at the pick with a cock of his head that was disturbingly similar to the posture of the one-eyed raven.

"Fine. Let's dig some more, then."

10.

Nick was disappointed to discover that the journal of Thaddeus Dekker was not a coherent account of his life, but merely a set of philosophical musings jotted down at odd times, probably so that the writer would not forget them. He lay in his pyjamas in the old iron bed on its squeaking mattress, his head propped up on two feather pillows, leafing through pages that smelled of mildew and dust. The electric lamp on the bedside table cast a pleasant yellow glow over the book. He had found nothing in the loose papers about the history of the farm. Some of the neatly penned notes in the journal pertained to Germanic or Scandinavian mythology, while others seemed to be fragments of a kind of ritual magic.

His heart rate quickened when he came across a crude drawing of the solar system spread across two of its pages. It showed unmistakably the same alignment of the planets with the moon that was to occur five nights hence. None of the New Age books in his library that talked about the Sumerian prophecy of the alignment was older than the 1970s. The clay tablets that described it had only been unearthed in 1953, and had not been deciphered for another twenty years. Yet clearly it must have been known from some other source in 1903, when Josiah Dekker's father wrote the journal.

He began to read passages at random to gain a flavour of the author's mind. It was crazy stuff, but interesting even so. Anyway, who was he to judge what was crazy? He had bought an abandoned farm and left his wife out of fear for the consequences of a pattern of lights in the night sky. Most people would call him crazy. Maybe he and the Dekkers had more in common then ownership of this farm.

"The wolf of fairytale is a poetic metaphor for something of great potency that is not easy to contain. Its closed jaws signify the power to restrain, but its open jaws the power to destroy. The chain that binds the wolf in myth is to be understood as lawful order that subdues the brutality of nature so that its random force cannot plunge the world into the chaotic vortex."

On the page facing this text was a pen drawing of a gigantic wolf with a chain around its neck. The other end of the chain was attached to a huge rock on the ground. A hero or god stood before the savage animal and extended his hand into the wolf's gaping jaws. There was a kind of halo around the head of the hero that framed his face. Written beneath the drawing were the words, "Fenrir the Devourer, Fenrir the Oath-Enforcer, Fenrir the Space-Eater."

Nick turned the page.

"Wotan of the One Eye is wisest of the Aesir. His two familiar spirits Huginn and Muninn haunt his path in the form of ravens, one named Thought and the other, Memory. It is significant that the wolf is not only Wotan's guardian spirit and clan beast, but also his greatest foe, whose power shall be unleashed at the Götterdämmerung, or Twilight of the Gods."

Below the text was drawn a line of the same twenty-four angular symbols that were engraved on the links of the iron chain, and scratched in pink chalk around the circle on the floor beside the bed in which he now lay reading.

"The runes are letters for writing, but more than this, they are symbols of realization. They bring forth into being that which is conceived, and also bind with their authority that which must be restrained until the proper hour of its unleashing."

Runes. That was the word Nick had been trying to remember. He had read about the runes in some of his books, while researching end-time prophecies. They were symbols of magic first used by ancient shamans among the tribes of German mercenaries that lived in northern Italy before the time of Christ. Over centuries they had spread across Europe to Scandinavia and England, and even as far west as Iceland. They held an evil reputation according to most authorities, and were linked with black magic and blood magic. The Dekker clan must have been a family of hereditary magicians, or hexenmeisters as they were called among the German immigrants. The runes could be used to heal, but also to blight or kill. He remembered reading something about bind-runes, where several runes were combined into a single symbol, but could not remember the details.

He turned the page.

"When the stars come right, the wolf is drawn from its lair where it sleeps the sleep of ages. The wind from the sea awakens it. Then must the wolf's bane be brandished. The horoscope will not occur during my term of life, but one who comes after me must be faithful to the ancient duty. The man-child in Sarah's womb may live long enough to see it, or if not him, then his son that follows after him."

Sarah, Nick guessed, was Thaddeus Dekker's wife. Josiah was probably Sarah's child. Thaddeus had no way to know that his son would be the end of the Dekker line. Nick continued reading from the yellowed page.

"The bitter well is only one knot in a complex web of threads or lines extending across the face of the terrestrial globe. Where these lay lines cross, there lie hid the engines of salvation. Most have been forgotten by humanity, but each has its caretaker who awaits the sounding of the cosmic bell in the heavens, which is misconceived by the biblical prophets as the trumpet of the archangel. Should one knot fail, the entire fabric will unravel, and the enemy will be victorious on the Day of Alignment.

"As the pattern of the stars begins to take shape, there will come an awakening of unrest throughout the nations of the world. Lawlessness and lust shall prevail over reason. Men shall rend their garments and run screaming through the towns, and dogs shall go mad. By these and like signs the music of the spheres announces itself, as it builds to the final ringing discord. Listen on the night wind when stars are joined in purpose."

On the next page was drawn the same symbol that was inscribed in white chalk in the middle of the circle on his bedroom floor. It appeared to be a bind-rune—a combination of various rune symbols joined together. There was some text on the facing page.

"Loki is the name given by the Northmen to the spirit of disorder and misrule. He is not a god, but a blind force of nature that seeks to increase the confusion and terror on which he feeds. Doubt is his drink, madness his meat. Some call him a demon of the flames. It is certain that he is a shape-shifter. Just as a shadow is nothing in itself, but appears to have form when outlined by the light of the sun, so Loki is himself empty of meaning, but gives the illusion of malicious purpose when in conflict with universal law, which frames and defines him."

Nick shut the journal. These were insane ramblings, the words of a man who had lost all contact with reality. They were giving him the willies. He shivered, wondering how close he was to a similar condition of incoherence. He wanted to dismiss Dekker's mad book from his mind, but the drawing of the planetary alignment haunted him. He could see it even when he closed his eyes to rest them against the glare of the bedside lamp. He wondered if Josiah Dekker had died in the very bed in which he now lay, on this same mattress, reading his father's journal. If so, how long had he lain here before the discovery of the corpse?

He opened his eyes to see Charlie Pye's round, smooth face surrounded by its circle of white curls, staring at him from no more than a foot away. Nick made an involuntary sound in his throat as he jerked his head back into the pillows. He stared around the bedroom. It was dark outside—he had not bothered to draw the curtains, and the window was a grid of black rectangles. The lamp was still turned on beside the bed. The journal of Thaddeus Dekker lay on the blankets between his parted knees. Had he fallen asleep?

"What are you doing here, Charlie?" he asked in a reasonable voice, and casually glanced down at the mute's hands. They were both empty. He swallowed with difficulty. His throat was dry.

Pye grinned and winced as he felt the twinge from his swollen lip. He motioned for Nick to get out of bed and follow him to the window. Nick did so.

"I don't see anything, Charlie," he said as he gazed at the black glass.

Pye moved back toward the bed and reached for the lamp.

"Don't turn that off—" Nick began.

The room went black. He could no longer see Pye. He looked toward the doorway but could not see it, either.

The hand on his shoulder made him jerk. He started to curse, then noticed a faint light coming through the window. It was a soft glow of many colors that moved and danced over the panes of glass. As his eyes adjusted to the darkness, he saw the faint outline of the other man reach for the sash and raise the lower half of the window.

There was no bug screen. Wonderingly, Nick bent his head and extended it out the opening.

The entire sky was aflame with pastel colours that danced in a waving curtain extending almost from horizon to horizon. It was the most spectacular instance of the aurora borealis he had ever seen. It was so bright, it illuminated the grass and the oak trees near the house. By its light he could see the clump of alders that marked the bitter spring on the far side of the field. He watched the rustling curtain of colors like a man in a trance. It was beautiful, yet in some solemn way terrifying. It almost drove the question from his mind—almost, but not quite.

He remembered locking the front and back doors before going to bed. How had Charlie Pye entered the house?

11.

In the morning, while Pye was occupied on a ladder, putting a new coat of white paint on the front of the house, Nick made a detailed examination of the windmill. He had been so busy with essential repairs to the house over the past few weeks that it was his first chance to really look over the archaic tower. A system of stairs and ladders gave him access to all its parts.

He was delighted to discover that its complex oaken and iron mechanism was intact. All it needed was cleaning and some axle grease, which he found in a sealed can in the barn. The canvas panels on the four great sails that circled above the barn had been treated with paint or some other kind of weather protection and were in surprisingly good condition, with only a few small rents where the wooden latticework beneath showed through.

The gearing at the base of the shaft continued to puzzle him. He decided that the iron spindle might have been used to drive some sort of machinery inside the barn—perhaps to run a sawmill. The odd thing was that the gears seemed designed to slow the turning of the spindle, not speed it up. This would give it more turning power, but would render it useless for running the blade of a circular saw. There was no evidence he could find that it had ever been employed to grind grain into flour, or even to lift bales of hay into the loft, although the iron spindle did suggest the latter function.

He left the barn around noon and made his way across the field toward the windbreak that separated his property from that of Hoffmann. It was not a visit he took pleasure in making, but Hoffmann was his closest neighbour, and he would have to live beside the man. He wanted at least to attempt some form of reconciliation before he let the soreness between them fester. And, he admitted to himself, there was another reason. He wanted to learn what Hoffmann knew about Charlie Pye.

The sudden appearance of Pye over his bed the previous night had shaken him. After pointing out the display of Northern Lights,

Pye had left the house, and in the morning Nick had come downstairs to find both front and back doors locked from the inside, just as he remembered leaving them. None of the downstairs windows were open. For some reason he could not define, he had felt uneasy about asking Pye how he had made his way into the house.

The pair of ravens that roosted on the roof of the barn for much of the day followed him into the trees. He heard their harsh croaks over his head as he walked through the cooling shadows. The stand of tall spruce trees had not been cut for half a century. They grew in a thick wall of interlocking boughs, but the undergrowth around their roots was sparse and made for easy walking, with only an occasional need to duck beneath a low-hanging branch. The thick bushes were at the edges of the windbreak, where the sunlight was able to reach them. He pushed his way through onto Hoffmann's land and saw the man's salmon-pink house beside a white barn, midway down a gently sloping field, with the blood-red banks of the Shubenacadie River winding in the background beyond it.

A shadow crossed his face. He felt a brush of feathers, and a loud croak sounded almost in his right ear. Instinctively he put up his arm, but the bird was already gone. He was half prepared when the other raven came at him from the opposite direction. It was close enough for him to see its small white eye as it dove at his face and veered away only at the last instant. This attack was repeated several more times, until Nick was able to find a rotting stick among the bushes. He waved it over his head, yelling in defiance. Either the weapon or his cry made the birds stop their attack. They perched high in the trees behind him and cawed loudly.

Like something out of an Alfred Hitchcock movie, Nick thought as he continued toward the house, shaking his head in disbelief. Neither bird had cut him, but the edges of their beaks were like razors and could have done some serious damage. He wondered if he should invest in a shotgun? He was philosophically against owning a gun, but could not let a couple of birds attack him whenever he stepped out of his house. He wondered if ravens were able to catch rabies.

Hoffmann's little two-story house was not in as good a state of repair as his barn. The barn looked almost new, but the house showed signs of rot at the eves and around the windowsills. There was no visible activity from either building. A silver Ford pickup truck sat beside the house on a patch of gravel, and he saw the tractor parked near the barn. The truck meant that Hoffmann was probably home, unless he'd been picked up by a friend in another vehicle, or owned a second vehicle himself.

Nick approached the front entrance and rapped on the wooden screen door with his knuckles. He waited, shifting his weight from one foot to the other on the planks of the low wooden step, which was close enough to the grass not to need a railing. The unpainted boards were covered in a fine layer of green algae, caused by the spring rains. Idly, he turned and let his gaze wander around the yard. He noticed an axe resting upright against an old chopping block, its blade orange with a recent patina of rust. He knocked again, more loudly, and listened. There was no sound from inside the house.

"Hoffmann? Hoffmann, are you in there?"

He walked out into the middle of the grass-covered yard and looked over at the barn. The doors were chained shut and padlocked on the outside, and there was no other way to enter. Hoffman was not in there. Returning to the house, he began to make a circuit around it. At the rear of the side facing the barn, the slanting exterior hatch to the cellar stood open. He approached the gaping opening with slow steps, listening for noises from inside. For some reason he felt uncomfortable, as though he were an intruder.

"Hoffmann?" he repeated loudly to announce his presence.

The cellar was quiet. He stopped at the edge of the opening. The angled doors of the hatch were made of plywood and had been left opened to either side. Inside the wooden framework of the entrance, a set of open wooden steps led down into a black interior. He put one leg into the opening on the top step, then hesitated. A rotten stench wafted up from the cellar on a vagrant eddy of wind and made him gag. No wonder the doors had been flung open, Nick thought. Some animal must have wandered in and died. Hoffmann was trying to air it out.

He stood undecided with one boot on the first step, feeling uneasy but not able to understand why. From the darkness below there came the lazy buzzing of flies.

"Screw it, I'll come back tomorrow," he muttered to himself.

Hoffmann was waiting when he rounded the corner to the front of the house. He wore the same denim overalls and chequered shirt, the same hunter-orange cap.

"Something I can help you with, Mr. Hanford?"

Nick shrugged.

"I just came over to say I hope there's no hard feelings about the other day."

"None on my part," Hoffmann said with an easy smile. "I should be the one to apologize. I shouldn't have hit your hired man."

"No, you shouldn't," Nick agreed. "But what's done is done."

"How is he working out for you?"

"He's a good worker. Doesn't shirk or complain." Nick hesitated. "He's a little odd at times."

"I expect he would be," Hoffmann agreed.

Nick looked at the spruce trees at the edge of the field. The ravens were nowhere in sight.

"I wonder if you would mind telling me what you know about him."

"He's a troublemaker," Hoffmann said, the smile gone from his face. "Always poking his nose where it isn't wanted, always getting involved in things that are none of his business."

"Is he—a local man?"

"About as local as I am."

"How did he lose his voice? Was he born that way?"

"Don't know about that. He's never spoken for as long as I've known him, that's all I can tell you."

"So you don't know his family."

Hoffmann's eyes seemed to glitter.

"I've never had the pleasure of their acquaintance."

Nick nodded. This was not getting him anywhere.

"One more thing. Have you ever had any trouble with birds?"

"What sort of trouble?"

"Have any birds ever attacked you?"

Hoffmann grunted in derision.

"Birds don't attack people. Why would they?"

Nick thought of telling him about the ravens, then decided there was no point.

"Well, I better go back to my place. Lots of work. Come over any time."

"I will do that."

It was only while he was walking back up the slope toward the trees that Nick realized he had not seen a single animal on Hoffmann's farm. Not a cow, not a horse, not a chicken, not even a barn cat. The animals must all be in the barn, he thought. But why was the barn locked?

12.

In the early evening, he took Earl LeBlanc's business card from the top of the fridge, where he had put it for safe keeping, and dialled the long-distance number written on the back. There was an hour difference between Nova Scotia time and Florida time. It was late enough that Judeth Marino should have finished her dinner, but not so late that she was likely to be in bed.

A man answered.

"I'd like to talk to Judeth," Nick told him.

"Yeah? What is it about?"

His voice had a Spanish accent. He must be the woman's husband, Nick thought.

"It concerns family business. It's in connection with the old farm her mother owned in Nova Scotia."

"That farm, it's already sold."

"I know. I'm the man who bought it."

There was a pause. Nick heard muffled conversation in the background, and the clink of silverware on china. They must dine late in the Marino household, he thought.

"Hello?" Her voice was uncertain, its tone chill.

"I'm sorry to interrupt your evening meal, Mrs. Marino," Nick said.

He explained who he was and how he had obtained her phone number.

"Thank you for sending the documents connected to the house. I really appreciate having them."

"It was nothing," she said, her voice a little warmer. "They were no use to me."

"Even so, it was a thoughtful thing to do."

There was silence for several seconds.

"Why did you call me, Mr. Hanford?"

"I've been going over the papers and the journal you sent, and I thought perhaps you could give me some background about their contents."

"I don't think so."

"But you have read the journal, haven't you?"

"Yes, I read it. But I didn't understand it."

Nick thought quickly, trying to put his questions in order.

"Was your great-uncle a hexenmeister?"

"Hex . . . what? What did you say?"

"Hexenmeister. It's a name for a German magician."

"I'm sorry, I don't recognize the word."

"Did you know your great-uncle when you were a child?"

"No, I never met him."

Nick pressed his lips together in frustration. He was getting nothing.

"Did your mother ever talk about him to you?"

The silence lasted so long, he thought the phone might have dropped the connection.

"My mother said very little about her uncle. Whenever I would ask about him, she refused to talk about him at all. Until the end, that is . . ."

"The end? The end of what?"

"My mother went senile and had to be placed in a nursing home here in Florida. I used to visit her twice a week."

"I'm sorry to hear it. That must have been hard on you."

She sniffed, declining his sympathy.

"You do what you have to do when the time comes."

"Yes, I suppose you do. Did she ever talk about the farmhouse?"

"She talked about everything, Mr. Hanford. She babbled nonstop about her childhood. She thought I was her dead sister. Toward the end she didn't recognize anyone."

"What did she say?"

"Just a lot of nonsense. She told me I must never sell the farm. She said it was a family trust—a sacred trust, she called it—and that disaster would befall me if I ever let it pass out of the family. She thought I was her sister when she said it—all my life, whenever I asked about the farm she wouldn't speak about it. But at the end when she didn't know who I was, she told me."

Nick paused to digest this information. It explained why Dekker's niece had kept the farm for two decades, even though it was unoccupied. She felt that she was under some sort of obligation never to sell it.

"Did your mother ever speak about an iron chain buried in the field beside the house?"

"An iron chain?"

"There was an old chain, like a ship's anchor chain, buried in the field. Did your mother ever mention it?"

"No. Never."

"What about the windmill? Did she ever say what it was used for?"

"She babbled something a few days before she died, but it was gibberish."

"What was it? Maybe it will mean something to me, even if it didn't mean anything to you."

"Hmm, let me think, now. She said, 'Always keep the gears greased and the sails mended. There's no time for regret when the wind rises.' That's what she said, I think."

"When the wind blows," Nick repeated.

"When the wind rises. And she said something else. I'd almost forgotten, it was so silly. She said, 'Watch the ravens. The ravens know when the wolf walks.' Does that mean anything to you?"

Nick felt his heart rate quicken. The ravens and the wolf had been mentioned in the journal of Thaddeus Dekker in connection with the mythology of the one-eyed god of the North, Wotan.

"I've got two ravens on my barn roof," he told her. "They watch me while I work."

"The Dekker farm has always had ravens, Mr. Hanford. I remember someone in the family—I forget who it was now—saying that the ravens have been there for generations."

Nick laughed uneasily.

"I wonder if they are the same pair of birds."

"Oh, I doubt that. They probably have a rookery somewhere close by."

He heard her husband's voice speak in the background in a demanding tone, but could not distinguish the words.

"I have to go, Mr. Hanford. There's something I must do."

"Of course, Mrs. Marino. I didn't mean to take up so much of your time."

"Not at all. I enjoyed speaking with you."

"Maybe I can phone you again at a more convenient hour?"

"I don't see what that would accomplish. I've told you everything I know about the old place. Except—I remember something else my mother said, but it's meaningless."

"Please tell me anyway."

"Well, she said, 'Beware the deceiver. Beware his smiling face. He comes as a helper wrapped in the wool of the lamb, but beneath it lie hidden sharp teeth and savage claws.' Or something like that. Does it mean anything to you?"

"Not really, but I'll think about it."

"You do that. Take care, Mr. Hanford."

"I always do," Nick said lightly.

"No, I mean it. Take care of yourself. The farm had a bad reputation in my family. It might have been some kind of duty or obligation to hang onto it, but nobody even liked to talk about it. Looking back all those years ago, I think they were afraid of the place."

"Afraid to visit it, you mean?"

"I mean they were afraid even to speak about it. I was only a child but I could see it in their eyes."

The male voice sounded in the background, this time more insistently.

"I really have to go. Goodbye."

He set the cell phone down on the table and looked at it thoughtfully.

13.

With the help of Charlie Pye, over the next three days Nick was able to clear the chain all the way up to the alders. He chopped a path through the dense little trees with his axe and hacked up the mat of interlocking roots. He discovered that alders have a curious property: their bleeding sap turns bright red after they are cut. The stumps of the trees resembled a pile of severed children's limbs. When at last he exposed the place where the chain entered the iron elbow at the edge of the spring, he felt an objectless but undeniable satisfaction. He could go no further in that direction.

He tried to pry up the pipe using a six-foot crowbar, but soon abandoned the effort. It was fitted between the boulders too cunningly, and the boulders themselves were too massive to move without heavy equipment. No matter how hard he pulled on the chain, he could not draw it through the pipe. It must be attached to something heavy beneath the black water, he decided. Maybe the fanciful anchor he sometimes visualized.

Nick turned his efforts in the other direction and began to dig along the chain toward the barn, with the unquestioning Pye helping him. The chain veered neither right nor left, but pointed directly at the barn doors. It was easier work, because as they neared the driveway the heavy links were buried closer to the surface. The purpose for the chain continued to vex him. He thought it might have been intended to conduct lightning away from the windmill and into the spring where it would do no harm, but this was only speculation. There was no lightning rod on the windmill.

Had anyone asked him why he was wasting so much time and effort exposing the chain, when in all likelihood he would just have to rebury it, Nick could not have answered. He found no reason to do this useless work that would justify it, even in his own mind, other than that the mystery of the chain intrigued him. Truth be told, it had become a minor obsession.

The open trench passed between the uprights of the barn door frame without hindrance. There was no threshold, and the floor of the barn was packed soil. The chain extended down almost the full length of the barn, to near the foot of the windmill shaft. Here, it did something unexpected—it bent from a straight line into a spiral that was around nine feet in diameter. Nick did not attempt to cheat by digging across the spiral, but uncovered its entire length all the way to its centre.

He knocked the last clumps of dirt off the end of the chain with the blade of his shovel and bent his back to study it with curiosity, while Pye looked on over his shoulder. The end was a kind of wrought-iron horn about a foot long that tapered toward its tip and curved gently. A line of runes ran along the side of the horn.

Nick looked at it for several minutes without touching it. Having exposed the entire chain from end to end, he found himself reluctant to disturb it from the trench. He decided to leave it lying where it was until he could take a detailed series of photographs, and ordered Pye not to move it. Then he returned to the house to wash up for supper.

The cellphone was ringing when he reached the back door. He hurried in and grabbed it up from the kitchen table.

"Nick? Is that you?"

"Pam?"

"I've been calling all day, trying to reach you."

There was uncharacteristic strain in her voice.

"I was outside, working."

"I had to tell you that I'm moving out of the condo and into Dora's parents' house. You remember my friend from the university, Dora Sims?"

Nick had an image in his mind of a small, mousy woman in wire glasses, with greying sandy hair that she always wore pulled back in a ponytail, as though she were in a perpetual state of arrested adolescence.

"It's getting bad in Montreal, Nick. Really bad, I mean. Have you seen the looting on the television?"

"I don't have a television. But I listen to national news on CBC Radio."

"The mayor is talking about shutting off the electricity to enforce the curfew. I think he's gone insane, Nick. Everyone's insane."

"Are you safe?"

"The burning and looting is mostly west of here. I'm going to stay one more night before I drive Dora to her parents' house outside the city. You can still drive a car on the streets during the daytime."

Nick suppressed his irritation. If only she had listened to him and come with him to Nova Scotia, she would be safe here on the farm. There was some scattered unrest in Truro but nothing more widespread. The worst of the insanity seemed confined to the major cities.

"It's the Sumerian Prophecy, Pam. I warned you about it."

"I know." Her voice was unemotional. "I should have listened, but I thought you were deluded."

"Are you seeing the aurora borealis at night?"

"Yes. It's spectacular—bright enough to read by. The police say we're not supposed to look at it. People do crazy things when they stare at it for too long."

This was something he had not heard on the radio.

"I can't reach you," he said. "They've cancelled all flights out of the Halifax Airport until further notice, and the Trans-Canada Highway is closed at the provincial border."

"I know. Thank God the phones still work. I don't expect you to come back, Nick, I just wanted to talk to you and let you know where I'm going."

"I'm glad you called," he said, voice suddenly gentle. "I miss you."

"I miss you, too."

He held the phone and looked at it, wondering what to say.

"What's going to happen, Nick?"

He found himself wanting to reassure her. Instead he said, "Nobody knows. The prophecy only predicts the chaos that builds before the Alignment. It says nothing about what happens after that."

"Are we all going to die?"

Hysteria was not far below the surface of her voice.

"I just don't know, Pam."

Her silence was more eloquent than words.

"I have to go now," she said.

"I love—"

The dial tone cut off his words. He set the phone gently back on the table.

14.

He decided to make one last quick run into Truro with the pickup before the day of the Alignment. He needed to buy galvanized nails to refasten some of the clapboards on the house. Many of the old nails had rusted clean through, and some boards were hanging in place out of force of habit alone. Assuming he still had a house after the Alignment passed, it was something that needed to be fixed. He also needed to fulfill his promise to Charlie Pye to buy him a kerosene stove for cooking.

The days were long this time of year, and he still had a couple of hours of light left. He figured that if he kept to the main roads in the city and went straight to the Home Hardware store and back, he would be safe enough.

He got into the truck and inserted the ignition key. A shadow fell across his face. He looked up and saw one of the ravens perched on the hood of the truck. The bird was enormous seen from this close. Nick held his breath and just admired it without moving. It was the same bird with the bad eye that had watched him from the alders while he examined the bitter pool. It walked back and forth along the hood of the truck, like an English naval officer with his hands behind his back, pacing the deck of his ship. Every now and then it stopped to cock its head at him and eye him through the windshield with its disturbingly penetrating single black eye.

Something thumped above his head, and he heard walking. The two birds were never far apart from each other.

"If you're looking for a free ride into town, I can't help you," he told the one-eyed raven on the hood.

Abruptly, it lunged forward and pecked with its long black beak at the windshield.

"Hey!" Nick shouted. He thumped his fist against the inside of the glass.

The bird hopped back and eyed him with a contemptuous tilt of its head. It cawed loudly once and spread its enormous wings. In an instant it was gone. He heard two more caws from somewhere behind the truck, near the barn.

"They must think they own this place," he muttered to himself as he turned the key.

The radio reports had not prepared him for what he found in Truro. Most of the side streets were barricaded. There were overturned cars, piles of smouldering tires emitting columns of black smoke that smelled of burnt rubber, and people running in packs from house to house with their arms full of stolen items. Pillars of smoke rose from burning houses. The main streets were open, but they were almost deserted, apart from a scattering of police and soldiers directing traffic. Fear was naked on their faces. The few cars that passed him were moving very fast. A fire truck blasted by on the opposite side of the road, its siren screaming.

It was evident that law and order had not broken down completely, but it was strained to its limit. He hated to imagine what it would be like when night fell.

He drove along Prince Street and turned down Willow Street. The little brown Home Hardware was located on the corner, surrounded by nice houses with well-kept yards. The lot at the side of the store was almost deserted. He pulled in and walked around to the front doors. When he tried them they rattled but did not open. Nick leaned close to the glass and peered into the store. An older man with thinning white hair and eyeglasses walked toward the entrance with a hesitant pace. He studied Nick through the doors for several seconds, then unlocked them to let him in.

"Sorry," he said. "We have to be careful lately."

"I understand."

The clerk locked up behind him.

"I saw some people looting houses," Nick told him.

He turned, and Nick saw the same fear in his eyes that had been in the eyes of the police. It was the stunned look of a deer that has been hit by a car, but doesn't know how to get off the highway—a mingling of confusion, shock, and a kind of dread.

"We probably shouldn't have opened today, but we didn't want to disappoint our customers."

Nick turned and saw a middle-aged women in glasses and a younger man near the back of the store.

"I won't take up much of your time."

He bought the nails, the cook stove, and a few other things he needed for the house. The elderly clerk locked the doors behind him as he left and stood inside the glass, peering nervously left and right.

Nick drove back the way he had come. At least he knew the streets he had just traversed were not blocked by barricades. As he went by the Pye Chevy dealership, he noticed a man in a suit with something in his hands, standing just inside the entrance to the lot. The dealership behind him looked closed up for the day. He recognized the man as Jim Michaels, the salesman who had sold him the truck, and slowed down to ask what he was doing, standing by himself in the middle of the parking lot. He rolled down the truck's window to holler across the street.

Michaels saw him and started to walk toward him on stiff legs. As he neared the street, Nick recognized what he had in his hands. A pump-action shotgun. He started to call out the man's name, when Michaels raised the gun and fired at the truck. It was a bad shot. One of the pellets from the shell cracked the mirror on the side of the door. The salesman's eyes were wide and empty, and spittle glistened on his chin. The lights are on, but nobody's home, Nick thought as he floored the gas pedal. The man raised the gun again but did not fire a second time. In his rearview mirror, through the back window on the cab of the truck, Nick watched him walk slowly back toward the center of the car lot.

Whatever was making people crazy, some were more susceptible to it than others. Maybe some were even immune to the effect. He didn't feel any different at all. Unfortunately, that didn't matter. The few who were unaffected could not stem the rising madness. Once a certain level of insanity was reached in society, it could no longer sustain itself and it came apart.

15.

The next day, the electricity failed. For most people living outside the towns that meant no water, but Josiah Dekker had planned for such inconveniences. The hand pump bolted to the rough planks of the counter by the kitchen sink ran to the same shallow dug well that served the piston pump in the cellar. There was no hot, but an endless supply of cold water for drinking, cooking, washing, and flushing. The cellphone went out of order at the same time as the electricity.

The Truro radio station he had been listening to for local news managed to stay on the air using generator power, and Nick was able to pick up the nervous announcers on his emergency AM-FM receiver, which was part of his survival gear. With shaking voices, they urged everyone to stay in their homes to avoid the rioting and remain calm. None of them seemed to know what was going on, although there were a few brief references to the prophecy of the planetary alignment that was to occur late tomorrow night.

In the short term Nick was not worried about the loss of power or the riots. He had adopted the habit of keeping the gas tank of the Accord full, and had another twenty gallons of gasoline in plastic five-gallon cans stored in the back of the pickup under a tarp. The shelves of the pantry off the kitchen held large bags of flour and rice, a twenty-pound sack of potatoes, a dozen cans of condensed milk, tea, coffee, packages of dried fruit, cans of beans, soup, corned beef, salmon, and other foodstuffs. It would be a month before he and Charlie Pye needed to worry about going hungry, maybe two months. There was ample firewood cut and stacked to keep the cook stove in the kitchen burning, and he had laid in a supply of batteries for the radio and the flashlights.

What worried him was what would happen after the Alignment. The unrest building up to the celestial event was only the preliminary manifestation of the full disaster foretold by the priest cast of Sumer. None of the commentaries were clear about what the Alignment itself would do to the world, but there was general agreement that it would be apocalyptic in scope. The prophecy described it in vague poetic terms as a moment of balance that might tip either way: If the evil unleashed by the Alignment were turned back by a mysterious class of beings known only as the Watchers, things would return to normal; but if it were not repelled at the time it was awakened, chaos would reign eternal.

Nick spent the afternoon reglazing the windows of the house while Pye continued with his painting. He had already managed to apply two coats of white paint to the front and was working on the first coat on the side. They both used ladders—Nick had found a pair of old wooden ladders hanging up in the barn. In order to stay out of the handyman's way, he worked on the windows opposite the side of the house Pye was painting.

The putty that held the panes of glass in place was as hard as concrete. Some of it fell away in pieces from the frame at a mere touch, leaving only the small metal glazing points to retain the panes, while other sections stuck so tight to the old wood that he had to chisel them off. It was hot, exacting work, preparing the frames for new beads of putty. The deer flies and the occasional enormous horsefly seemed to regard his exposed skin as a buffet laid out for their dining pleasure.

Nick wiped the sweat from his eyebrows with the back of the bent wrist that held his putty knife and looked down from the second-story window he worked on to the trench crossing the field. From the ladder it was easy to see that the trench cut a completely straight line from the barn to the clump of alders. Now that the spiral ending of the chain inside the barn had been exposed, he could have dragged it out of its trench and gathered it up in one place beside the bitter spring, where it would be out of the way, but for some reason he felt no need to do so. Exposing the chain to the light of day had ended the odd obsession that had gripped him since discovering it.

He squinted at the stubble in the field. There was a variation in the colour of the close-cropped grass and weeds that he had not before noticed. It ran in a line past the bend of the gravel driveway that led into the barn. The grass on one side of this line was greener than on the other side. He traced it with his eye and realized that it curved in a large circle over the field, with the clump of alders at its centre.

This circle of yellowed grass and weeds did not quite reach the driveway. The house and barn lay outside it.

It almost looked as though the grass inside the circle were half-dead. Nick remembered Hoffmann's talk about crops blighted by the water of the spring when Dekker had tried to use it for irrigation. The difference was faint—so faint that he had never noticed it while walking in the field—but once seen, it was undeniable. He inverted the putty knife and used its butt to scratch his scalp. The water of the spring was bitter. He wondered if there was something it in—maybe arsenic—that made it a slow poison.

He descended his ladder and walked around the house. Pye was up his ladder, painting the eave near its peak. Nick called to him, and the mute paused his work.

"Take a look at the field, will you, Charlie?"

Pye looked out over the mowed field.

"Do you see a big circle there where the grass is browner? Takes up almost the whole field with the alders at its centre."

Pye squinted, then looked down at him and nodded.

"Do you know what causes it?"

Pye shrugged his shoulders and smiled in apology.

"Forget it, Charlie. Keep painting. You're doing a good job."

16.

It was just as well that Nick found it impossible to sleep that night. For several hours he studied the journal of Thaddeus Dekker, trying to make sense of its enigmatical observations. What was written there was plain enough to read, and even to understand; it was its application to the real world that eluded him. What was the meaning to these cryptic passages the old hexenmeister had penned out with such obvious care?

When at last he turned off the lamp on the bedside table and rolled over to try to sleep, it must have been near midnight. A yellow flicker caught his eye on the wall. He rolled back and realised it was coming from the window. He decided to get up and look at the aurora borealis for a while. It was impossible to predict the time of its appearance, but every night it seemed more intense than the night before. It only lasted for an hour or so when it came, but it was worth the wait.

The flicker did not come from the sky, but from the opened doors of the barn. He blinked and peered through the window panes, which were foggy with oil from the new putty he had used to reglaze them. He wondered what Pye was doing with a lantern so late at night. His eyes widened. Cursing, he pulled up the window sash and stuck his head out. The glow was too irregular to be caused by a lantern. His nostrils flared as they caught the acrid tang of smoke.

A shadow walked casually through the barn doorway. It stopped just outside with the flicker of the flames on its back and looked up at his window, as though it could feel his gaze. The light was bad. At first Nick was not even sure it was a man, but as he stared at the shadow, it seemed to become clearer, and for a moment he thought he recognised the skinny frame and rat-like face of the teenager who had thrown the chair at the plate glass window of the Chevy dealership. The shadow figure wavered and rippled uncertainly. Nick blinked hard and rubbed his eyes with his thumb and index finger to clear them. The fire inside the barn flared brighter. It was not the teenager, but Hans Hoffmann. The stocky farmer stood looking at Nick for several seconds. He raised his left hand and extended his middle finger upward.

"Hey!" Nick shouted.

With a grin, Hoffmann loped across the field toward the windbreak and was soon beyond the glow from the fire that burned inside the barn.

Nick stood frozen in place. A shiver of dread ran down his spine. The sound of something falling inside the barn finally set him into motion. He ran downstairs and grabbed the portable fire extinguisher he had bought for the kitchen. There was no point in fussing with the rubber hose that hung from a bracket at the corner of the house: without the pump to raise the water pressure, it was useless. Nor was there any point in trying to call the fire department. The cellphone was still out.

When he reached the barn, he almost turned back at the doorway. The fire blazed in the loft, concentrated on several old bails of hay, but sparks and burning matter had started to sift down between cracks in the loft floor and were igniting dry straw on the lower level. The sight of Charlie Pye, sprawled at the foot of the loft ladder wearing only white boxer shorts, made him enter. He put his arm up to shield his face from the heat. Dropping the fire extinguisher, he dragged Pye out of the barn by the heels and left him lying in the driveway.

He went back and climbed the loft ladder awkwardly with the metal cylinder of the little fire extinguisher in one hand. The heat almost knocked him off the ladder when he reached the top, but he held on with the crook of one elbow and sprayed the extinguisher back and forth across the floorboards of the loft. The white gas from the extinguisher was surprisingly effective. It killed enough of the fire for him to get up into the loft. He expended the rest of its contents putting out what was left of the burning straw and the places where the floorboards had caught, but he was able to smother the fires that had started on the ground level with his cotton pyjama top, which he took off and balled up in his hand for the purpose.

It was only after he was certain the fire was completely out that he left the barn to examine the condition of Charlie Pye. He found the round-faced little man sitting up on the gravel with his legs crossed and his head cradled in his hands. Blood trickled from a gash in his forehead.

"Are you all right, Charlie?"

The little man lifted his head and looked at Nick. There was a keenness in his grey eyes that Nick had not seen before. He nodded.

"Do you know what happened?"

Pye shook his head, pale eyes still fixed on Nick.

"Did Hoffmann hit you?"

Pye shrugged and put his hands together palm to palm, then laid his head across them and closed his eyes.

"You mean you were asleep?"

The little man nodded.

"It was Hoffmann," Nick said, as much to himself as to Pye. "He tried to burn down the barn. He must be insane."

The coloured lights of the aurora borealis started to dance in the starry blackness above. Pye looked up and smiled at Nick. He lay back on the gravel of the driveway with his hands folded behind his head. Nick watched him for a time, then knelt on the ground and stretched himself out beside Pye.

17.

After breakfast the next morning, Nick took the walk across the field and through the windbreak to Hoffmann's farm. The sky was overcast with featureless grey cloud. He had planned for years to view the celestial alignment that would occur this evening. It would be a fine joke of fate if it was cloudy and he could not see it. Still, he reasoned, at any given hour it had to be cloudy somewhere in the world. Why not here?

Inside the left sleeve of his beige golf jacket he carried a length of galvanised steel pipe that extended from his wrist to his elbow. He cradled the weight of it on his curled fingers as he walked. There was no way to know Hoffmann's mental state, but he had obviously been crazy last night, and Nick had no intention of facing him unarmed. The phone and electricity were both still off. The radio reported widespread looting and destruction of property in Truro, as well as random acts of violence. This made him give up the idea of driving in to the police station to report Hoffmann. Nick could only imagine how bad it must be in larger cities. He hoped Pamela was safe with her friends.

The ravens were there in the trees, but this time they did not attack him as he started down the slope to Hoffmann's house. They merely watched in silence. The one with the cataract tilted its head so that it could follow his progress with its good eye. Approaching the house across the grass with a slow step, Nick had time to regret not buying a dog. Its presence at his side would have been reassuring.

Common sense counselled him to leave the crazy Hoffmann to himself until the police could be reached. He was in no mind to listen to such sensible advice. After the stunt Hoffmann had pulled last night, he wanted an explanation. No, that was not true, he thought—he wanted a confrontation. The son of a bitch had tried to burn his barn, and he might easily have killed Charlie Pye, who was still recovering from the blow on the head.

Nothing had changed from his last visit. The silver Ford pickup was in the same place in the driveway. He could not tell if it had been moved or not. There were no animals outside. The double doors of the white barn were still padlocked. Taking a deep breath to steady his nerves, he stepped up on the wooden platform in front of the door of the house and knocked. The interior behind the door was silent. He banged harder, then opened the wooden screen door and tried the doorknob of the panel door. Few country people bothered to lock their houses, and Hoffmann was no exception. The door opened easily.

The house had a musty atmosphere, as though it had not been aired for weeks. He sniffed. There was also a rotten smell. He followed it to the kitchen, and opened the refrigerator. Without electricity, the meat and milk had not fared well. The steaks in the upper freezer section almost looked as though they had been rotting for weeks. He shut the freezer door with a wry face and moved on cautiously into the parlour, then looked into the downstairs bedroom, where evidently Hoffmann slept, and the bathroom. All the rooms on the main floor were deserted.

He glanced out the windows to see if the farmer were approaching the house from the driveway, then shifted his grip on the length of pipe and climbed the steep staircase to the upper level. The two small bedrooms above looked well lived-in, with clothes and possessions scattered about. For the first time it occurred to Nick to wonder if Hoffmann had a family. If so, they were not at home. He searched around the rooms but found nothing that might explain the farmer's crazy behaviour. Descending the stairs with slow steps, he went outside.

He started toward the locked barn, but stopped when he noticed that the hatch to the cellar was still wide open. He approached it and raised his right arm to breathe through the fabric of his jacket sleeve. The stench from inside the darkness had not improved. If anything, it was more concentrated.

"Hoffmann, are you down there? I'm coming down."

He let the pipe slide from his sleeve into his left hand. Its weight and the coolness of the galvanised steel against his fingers reassured him. With his back crouched, he descended the cellar steps sideways, ready to strike out with the pipe if attacked. At the bottom of the steps, he stood for a time with his hand across his mouth and nose, trying not to gag. The smell was indescribable. When his eyes began to adjust to the dimness, he walked deeper under the house.

In a corner near the oil furnace he found the body of a man, partially wrapped in a sheet of clear plastic, which was covered with flies and ants. The flies rose in a buzzing cloud and tried to get into Nick's mouth and nostrils as he batted them aside. Using the toe of his boot, he rolled the corpse over at the shoulder. Nick did not know what a corpse was supposed to look like after it had been dead for several weeks, but he was pretty sure this was it. The swollen, blackened face had been partly devoured by rodents and maggots. Both eyes were eaten out of their sockets. He did not recognise what was left and wondered if Hoffmann had shared his house with a brother, or if he had murdered some neighbour or a complete stranger who happened to knock at his door.

He shivered and decided he had spent enough time standing alone in the dark, looking at the half-eaten, fly-blown face of the corpse. If he were in a horror movie, he thought to himself, now was the moment the lunatic Hoffmann would leap out at him from behind the water heater with an axe. To his surprise and relief, this did not occur.

He left the cellar and stood trembling under the leaden sky, breathing deep lungfuls of clean air as he eyed the locked doors of the barn with loathing in his heart. He knew that he had to go over and force those doors open, but he dreaded what he would find. He glanced wistfully toward the windbreak, wishing he could just walk up the slope and into the trees and forget everything he had seen. The ravens were still perched on the crowns of two tall spruce trees, silently watching him with their knowing eyes. After standing for a minute or so, he stiffened his spine and made his way across the grass with reluctant steps.

18.

The stench grew stronger as he approached the small white barn. While he remained near the house, the breeze that blew across the slope from the mouth of the river had forced the smell back, but not even the breeze could prevent it from reaching his nose when he got within a dozen paces of the padlocked doors. He swallowed bitter saliva that made his stomach roll, and tried to ignore the taste.

Threading the galvanised pipe through the chain, he began to wind it like a propeller. The padlock parted with a snap of broken metal. He slid the chain from the brackets and swung open one side of the double door. The rotten smell of death washed over him like an invisible river. He coughed and spat, felt cold sweat break forth on his face and his stomach muscles contract. Vomit erupted from between his lips as he twisted his head to the side. It splashed down the edge of the door. He waited with his hands on his knees, bent forward, until his stomach emptied itself, then spat the foul acid taste out of his mouth and wiped his lips with the sleeve of his jacket. For several seconds he stood still. His entire body trembled as though shivering with cold, despite the mildness of the day. He took a step back and crouched to carefully wipe his jacket sleeve against the clean grass.

Time for a little fresh air and sunlight, he thought.

Even with both doors braced wide open with the smooth beach stones that rested in the grass for that purpose, it was still dim within the barn. Some light came through the cracks between the wide vertical boards that sided the structure. He took a deep breath and stepped over the threshold. A dozen rats ran out, two of them passing between his legs. They made no sound. The silence was absolute, and eerie. He blinked as his eyes adjusted to the gloom.

Rows of animal carcasses had been strung up on hooks from ropes tied around traverse beams. They swung gently in the breeze that managed to find its way through the opened doors. The dirt floor beneath them was bloody and piled with viscera and connective tissue. Nick recognised cows, a horse, and what looked like pigs and goats. Not all of them were in the same condition. Some were several weeks old, but others were fresher. Flies swarmed over them, and wriggling white maggots fell from them like grains of rice. The smell was unbelievable, unlike anything he had ever experienced. It made what he had smelled in the cellar seem like a flower shop. He forced his legs to carry him into the centre of the barn and stood with the carcasses hanging all around him.

They had not been butchered. Whatever had rent through their hides and disembowelled them, it had not been the blade of a knife. They were slashed open, as though by the claws of some big cat, or maybe a bear. He stopped his breath and leaned closer to study one maggot-encrusted slab of what he took to be beef, and frowned in disbelief. The blackened, dried meat had been gnawed by large teeth. The bite marks were enormous. Hoffmann had been feeding some kind of wild animal on his livestock over a period of weeks, and he had been letting the beast, whatever it was, do the killing. The throats of the inverted farm animals had been torn out. No wonder the floor of the barn was soaked in dried blood.

He looked around at the shadows in the stalls on either side and listened for movement, but saw and heard nothing. Stepping back, he peered up at the loft. It was possible the animal was still here. He had to be sure. With the length of pipe in his hand, he climbed the ladder to the loft and extended his head above the level of the loft floor. It looked deserted, and he saw no signs that a large beast had been kept there. To make sure, he climbed all the way up and checked behind the hay bales. Nothing. He descended and searched with care around the floor of the barn for dung. He found nothing that resembled the droppings of a large cat. If Hoffmann had kept the animal in the barn he must have cleaned up after it with care—which made no sense. Why would he clean up its droppings, but leave the offal from the slaughtered animals lying on the floor?

The fresher carcasses were smaller. It looked as though Hoffmann had let his horse and his cows be killed first, and then moved on to the pigs and lastly the goats. The most recent kills were at the far end of the barn where the light was dim. He stepped gingerly between the gently swinging carcasses, trying to avoid brushing against the squirming maggots while at the same time keeping his feet out of the rotting viscera beneath them. They were all half-gnawed. Whatever Hoffmann had been feeding in the barn, it requires fresh meat and would not eat what was rotten.

There was something about the last row of carcasses in the shadows at the end of the barn. The buzzing flies that swarmed in the air, rising from the rotten meat as he brushed past, seem to scold him for disturbing their feast. He brushed them off his face with his free hand and approached the final row with leaden feet. They were longer than goats, thinner than pigs. At first his eyes could make no sense of their torn skin and the dried, blackened blood that covered them. When he finally saw what they were, they seemed to jump into focus, and then he could not unsee. A mature and fleshy woman, a young man, and a girl no more than fifteen, hanging by their heels, naked, disembowelled, throats torn out, flesh missing from their thighs, buttocks and arms, dried and blackened blood covering the rest.

The carcass on the end twitched and shuddered. Nick dropped the galvanised pipe from numb fingers but did not notice. He stared at the bloodied body, his jaw slack, then moved around to see its face. Its eyelids fluttered, and suddenly it became a woman. Her long grey hair hung down to the floor, entangled in what had spilled from her gaping belly. The intestines still glistened and pulsed with life. Her lips moved. Against his will, he found himself crouching to bring his face level with hers.

"Did your husband do this?"

She whispered something. He bent his ear closer.

"He's . . . not my husband."

A low growl shook the barn. Nick jumped to his feet and stared around at the shadows, then realised the sound had come from outside through the wide gaps between the barn boards. A shadow rippled across the eastern wall, outlined by the vertical bars of sunlight shining through the cracks. It was enormous and walked on four legs. It stood still and he heard snuffing noises, like those made by a dog. Another deep growl rumbled from its throat. The sound awoke a primordial dread in Nick that was so basic, it almost took away his ability to stand. On slow, stalking steps the shadow moved along the wall toward the end of the barn with the wide open doors.

A shadow crossed that of the beast. It was like a great sail that swooped and spun away. He heard a croak. A second flying shadow flashed down from the opposite side. The beast stopped and ducked its head, roaring in fury until the wall of the barn rattled. The shadow birds, each as large as a small plane, attacked the giant shadow beast with unrelenting fury, until at last it whirled in its tracks and leapt away. Nick heard three triumphant croaks. The barn was silent once again.

He looked back down at the old woman. Her eyes were still open but there was no life in them. A fly settled on her lower lip and crawled into her mouth.

He crept out of the barn on the toes of his work boots, glancing all around for Hoffmann and his murderous pet, but the farm seemed deserted once more. The madman had probably fled. He had not taken his own truck because he retained enough of his reason to know it would be identified by the police. He must have left the predatory beast behind to feed on what remained of his family. Naturally. He could not take such a creature with him on the road.

Nick wished he had managed to get a better look at it. The sunlight shining through the cracks must have distorted its size and made it appear impossibly large. Lucky for him the ravens had driven it away. Ravens were carrion birds. They probably wanted what they could smell in the barn for themselves. These thoughts passed through his mind as he climbed the grassy slope and entered among the spruce trees of the windbreak.

19.

While walking back from the Hoffmann farm, Nick decided not even to try to tell Charlie Pye about the corpses. There was nothing to be gained by it. Pye already knew Hoffmann was a dangerous lunatic to be avoided. When the phone link was restored, he would call the nearest detachment of the Mounties and let them deal with it. Assuming the phone ever was restored. Assuming the world did not come to an end tonight. He did not dare drive into Truro to report the murders. According to the radio, there were violent riots going on in the city and all the surrounding towns, multicar pile-ups on the highways, suicides, murders, arsons. He made his way toward the house to tune in to the latest news and see if things were still getting worse.

Pye was not up his ladder, painting, so Nick assumed he must be in the barn. He walked around the corner of the house and went in through the back door to the kitchen, but stopped midway with one leg over the threshold. Pamela sat at the kitchen table, a steaming cup of coffee in front of her.

"Pam, what are you doing here?"

She smiled nervously and stood up. She wore a wrinkled navy-blue business suit with a bright red scarf around her throat. Her face looked strained beneath her makeup. There were dark shadows under her eyes.

"That's a hell of a way to say hello."

"Why didn't you tell me you were coming?" he said, stepping quickly forward to embrace her. She returned his hug with urgency and they kissed. It was surprisingly prolonged. His wife had not kissed him that way for more months than he cared to count.

"No phone, remember?" she said in a husky voice when their lips parted.

"But you said you were going to stay with Dora Sims at her parents' place outside the city."

She shrugged in his arms.

"That plan fell through. There were a few flights running out of Montreal, so I took the first one east and tried to rent a car at the Halifax Airport. No luck. There was a bus running to Truro and I managed to catch it."

"How did you get here from Truro?"

She showed him her hand and stuck out her thumb.

"I hitched."

He shook his head, laughing with her.

"If only I'd know you were coming, I could have picked you up in the Accord."

"It doesn't matter, I'm here now."

"Thank God you are. Now I know you're safe. Whatever comes tonight, we'll ride it out and put the pieces together tomorrow."

They sat at the table and sipped coffee while she told him about the ordeal of trying to get from Quebec to the East Coast. It had been a nightmare of long line-ups and delays, with the nerves of travellers and airport staff alike frayed to the breaking point.

Nick turned on the radio. The situation in and around Truro was getting worse. Dozens of house fires blazing out of control because the overtaxed fire service could not go to them. There were barricades across many downtown streets, and gang fighting had broken out in some neighbourhoods. At least several people had been shot during the looting of the previous night, which was dying down because there was nothing left to steal. They heard about ten minutes of news before the shaking voice of the young news reader cut off in midsentence.

"They must have lost their power at the station," he speculated.

He tried tuning across the dial, but no other station was active within range of the receiver. A rattle and bang came against the side of the house. Pamela looked up from her cup and arched her dark eyebrows in inquiry.

"That's my hired man, Charlie Pye," Nick explained with a smile. "Want to meet him?"

She returned the smile weakly but shook her head.

"I'll meet him later. Right now, would you mind if I lie down and get some sleep? I'm really exhausted."

He stood quickly.

"No, of course not, go upstairs and lie down on the bed. You must be worn out." He looked around the kitchen. "I'll carry up your suitcase."

"I already took it up," she told him.

They climbed the stairs and Nick followed her into the main bedroom. She stepped around the circle of chalk on the floor and pointed at it with a grimace.

"The previous owner must have had funny ideas about interior decorating."

"It's a long story," he said. "You get some sleep and I'll tell you all about it when you wake up."

Nick wondered if he should describe to her the horrors he had discovered at the Hoffmann farm, but decided it would serve no purpose, and would probably keep her awake. She was exhausted— let her sleep. He left her to go talk with Pye.

The ladder at the side of the house was empty once more, so he made his way into the barn. Pye sat on the floor at the rear, in front of the geared mechanism of the windmill. His back was to the open doors. He sat hunched over, as though holding something. It almost looked as though he were cradling a baby in his arms.

"What have you got there, Charlie?" Nick asked in a cheerful voice.

Pye looked over his shoulder. His pale, round face bore a solemn expression. The halo of white curls gave him an appearance of almost childlike innocence. As Nick approached, he lifted his hands. On them rested the elongated section of curved iron that formed the end of the chain. Nick saw that Pye had been cleaning it with a rag to get the dirt off it. He bent and gave it a closer look.

"It almost looks like a little statue, doesn't it?"

Pye nodded.

Nick ran his eye along its domed end where the last link of the chain was forged on, down its more slender free end, which was gently curved. The shape reminded him of something, but he could not bring it to mind.

Pye laid the chain on the ground and put his hands into his armpits, then flapped his elbows up and down, staring at Nick.

"That's what it reminds me of," Nick said. "It looks like a bird's head. That curved part is the beak. Damned if it isn't a raven's beak."

Pye nodded vigorously. He raised the end of the chain once again and held it out to Nick.

"What do you want me to do with it, Charlie?" Nick asked in puzzlement.

Pye merely motioned with the chain as though he wanted Nick to take it.

"I don't know what you want, Charlie. Can you show me what you mean?"

An expression of sadness came into Pye's face. He shook his head and lowered the chain slowly to the ground. Nick patted him on the shoulder awkwardly.

"It doesn't matter. We'll figure it out."

20.

The rain started before twilight. There would be no observation of the planetary alignment tonight. Nick covered his telescope with its waterproof tarp and tied it down tight. The wind was picking up. It looked as if there might be a storm coming. He left Pye putting away his painting tools and the ladders in the barn, and went into the house to see if Pamela was awake. Each time he had looked in on her, she had been deep asleep on top of the bed. The ordeal of the trip must have completely exhausted her.

He climbed the stairs with care, trying to keep the old treads from squeaking more than necessary. He saw that the effort was wasted when he reached the open bedroom door—she was sitting up, reading Thaddeus Dekker's journal by the light of a kerosene lantern, which she must have lit herself. She had found one of his pyjama tops to put on for sleepwear.

"This is some crazy shit," she told him, turning the book so that he could see the drawing of the Fenrir wolf.

"I know. The whole Alignment Prophecy is crazy, but here we are living it."

"You were right and I was wrong."

He said nothing. He knew how much that admission must have cost her pride.

"When it's over tomorrow, are things going to get better, or worse?"

"That I don't know," he said in a dry tone.

The top two buttons on the pyjama top was undone. He found himself staring at the shadow on her skin between the parted sides of the top and licked his lips. He realised that he wanted her. She seemed to sense his rising desire and smiled. Setting the book on the bedside table, she turned down the covers of the bed to reveal her bare thigh.

"Well come on," she said.

They made love with a passion they had not felt since the first year of their marriage. She positioned herself on top, even though she knew he did not particularly enjoy that position. He tried to roll her gently over but she resisted, so he let her have her way. While the rain hissed against the glass of the darkening window, she rode him to ecstasy and exhaustion. Afterwards, they lay side by side without speaking, and he fell asleep.

A rumble of thunder woke him. The rain beat furiously against the window in wind-driven sheets. Full night had fallen. How many hours had passed, he had no way to estimate. He felt the other side of the bed and realised that Pam had already gotten up.

"Pam?"

There was no answer from the bathroom. She must have gone down to the kitchen for something to eat, he thought to himself as he lit the kerosene lantern with a wooden match. Its brightly glowing mantle filled the bedroom with light. He found his clothes and boots where he had thrown them off and got dressed. As he was going out the door, he looked at the floor and stopped. The central chalk symbol in the circle was scuffed so that he could barely distinguish its traces. Pam must have done it by accident while wandering around in the darkness in her stocking feet, he thought. Just as well he had copied the circle and its symbol into his notebook. He wondered what thoughts Pam might have about the purpose for the circle, and decided to ask her.

His wife was not in the kitchen, or anywhere else in the house. A little tickle of worry started at the back of his mind, but he reasoned she must have gone to the barn to introduce herself to Charlie Pye.

He found his notebook where he had put it away in a kitchen drawer, pulled on his beige golf jacket, and went out to see if she was in the barn. The wind almost ripped the aluminum screen door out of his hand, but he caught it and forced it shut behind him. He slipped the notebook into an inside vest pocket of the jacket to protect it from the intensifying rain. When he walked around the corner of the house, he saw that he had been correct: a lantern glow was coming from the opened doors of the barn, which were latched back against the wind.

Lightning split the sky with blinding whiteness that illuminated the mountainous storm clouds scudding across the heavens on the gale. Nick stopped and stared upwards in disbelief. In that instantaneous flash he had seen something between the clouds. Thunder boomed in answer to the lightning. As he stood fixed in place with the rain pelting his cheeks, another bolt electrified the night from cloud to cloud, and he saw it again. Or was it merely a mountainous plume that roiled and writhed in the wind, lit from behind by the lightning? The crack of thunder almost knocked him from his feet, it came so close on the heels of the flash.

He flipped up the collar of his jacket and hurried across the grass and along the curving driveway to the barn. The chain trench was already full of water. As he drew nearer he saw someone stretched out just inside the open doors.

"Pam!"

He ran forward. His wife lay sprawled face down on the muddy gravel. She raised her head from her arm and focused her blinking eyes on his face. Her expression changed from confusion to relief.

"Nick, thank God you came. He attacked me. He tried to rape me and when I fought him off, he hit me."

He looked closer. A distant flicker of lightning revealed an ugly purple bruise on the side of her face and a trickle of blood from the corner of her ear.

"Who attacked you?" His thoughts ran wildly. It could only be that maniac Hoffmann.

"That, that," she said, gesturing into the barn.

He stared where she pointed and realised that Charlie Pye was sitting on the ground with his back to them, as he had sat earlier when Nick had talked to him.

"No," he told her. "Charlie would never do that."

"He attacked me," she said, a note of hysteria near the surface of her voice. She pulled her long hair away from her cheek. "He did this to me."

Nick blinked in confusion, wondering how to respond.

"You've got to restrain him," she said. "He might attack us again. He's a lunatic."

Hesitantly, he rose to his feet and approached Pye. The little man sat rocking in the middle of the spiral of the trench, cradling the end of the chain in his hands, just as he had before. When Nick stepped around him, he saw that Pye's face streamed with tears, even though his expression remained serene. Pye noticed Nick's shadow where it was cast by the lantern across the chain and raised the sculpted end to offer it to Nick.

"Charlie, look at me," Nick said carefully as he stood over him. "Did you hurt Pam?"

Pye's eyes widened. He shook his head vigorously.

"Did you try to rape her?"

Another shake of the head.

Nick realised that his wife had gained her feet and was approaching with slow steps. He motioned her away with his hand, but she ignored the gesture. He looked at her and felt a shiver of uncanny dread. He had never seen such an expression on his wife's pale features and would not have believed any human being could make such a face. It was like a chalk mask from the slits of which blazed frozen stars. In the lantern light he saw the glitter of her barred teeth when her lips parted.

"Pam, let me handle this."

"You should kill him for what he did to me," she hissed.

Nick shook his head with an instinctive motion, as though to clear it. Her voice was deep, harsh. Too deep and too harsh. It did not even sound like his wife. Lightning flashed, illuminating the outline of her body—but more than this, the outline of something that surrounded her, a kind of shadow that did not show in the flame from the lantern. It was irregular and enveloped her like a halo of black smoke. The instant the flash died, it was gone. Thunder rolled from somewhere over the river.

She stopped just outside the curve of the spiral trench and stood leaning forward, clenching and relaxing her hands at her sides, her red lips writhing away from her teeth in primal fury while she made animal sounds in her throat.

"Pam, you're not well. The blow to your head did something—"

"Kill him, you fool! Kill him before he kills the both of us!"

Nick looked down at Pye. The little man extended the end of the chain to him. Without even knowing what he intended, Nick took it. The chain was heavy in his hands. The end piece was almost a foot in length and solid wrought iron.

"That's it," his wife shrieked. "Use it on him. Dash out his brains."

Another flash illuminated the strange cloud that clung to her body. It was larger than before and seemed to rear up over her and extend forward, like the hooded head of a cobra. Then it was gone. The thunder rolled.

An eerie calmness poured into Nick through the top of his head. It felt like cool well water, and washed down over his nerves and muscles, filling the inside of his body. Pye's pale grey eyes seemed to glow with their own radiance as he stared at Nick.

"You want me to do something with this?"

Pye nodded solemnly.

"But you can't tell me or show me what I must do?"

Pye nodded again.

"What the fuck are you talking about?" Pam roared in a voice that did not even remotely resemble the voice of his wife.

Nick ignored her. The answer was close at hand. He felt it, drawing him. He was meant to do this. Some part of him realised in a distant way that he had always been meant to do this. His eyes fell on the iron spindle beneath the gears of the windmill.

The thing that was not Hans Hoffmann and not his wife Pamela shrieked in fury.

"Can it injure me?" he asked Pye.

The little man shook his head.

Of course not. Otherwise, it would already have killed him. He remembered making love a few hours earlier and tasted stomach acid in his mouth. He swallowed it down. The being that resembled his wife laughed mockingly.

"Was it good for you, Nick?" it said in a masculine voice. "It was good for me."

He studied the small slot in the middle of the iron spindle and compared its shape with that of the beak on the raven's head. Of course. It was so obvious, so simple.

The Pamela-thing lunged toward the lantern. With startling quickness, Charlie Pye got there first and snatched the lantern out of its reach. He put it on the ground behind him and confronted the threatening creature.

"Do you think you can stand against me?" it asked in a mocking tone.

The two grappled. Nick started toward them, then forced himself to remember that the creature who wore his wife's shape was not his wife. Pam was safe on the Sims' farm in rural Quebec. He returned his attention to the spindle.

Something was happening in the night sky outside the doors of the barn. It was more than just the storm. Lights, shapes, colours were moving above the clouds. Where the wind rent them apart, this higher cosmic display showed itself. With a part of his mind, Nick was aware of it gathering its force in the heavens as the Alignment reached its perfection, but he did not look at it. Instead, he dragged the heavy chain out of its spiral trench and over to the shaft of the windmill. He fitted the point of the raven's beak into the slot in the spindle and drove it home with the heel of his hand.

21.

The self-assurance Nick experienced when the black iron beak clanked into place on the iron spindle surprised him. It just felt right. More than this, in some weird way it felt familiar, as though he had done it before. Maybe in a dream, he thought.

The Pamela-thing was losing coherence as it struggled with whatever was the being he had known as Charlie Pye. As parts of its female shape faded into black smoke, Pye's body merely glowed more brightly. Even his clothing glowed. It was obvious to Nick that the Pamela-thing was stronger. It began to bear Pye backward, bending his spine into a tighter and tighter curve until his white curls almost brushed the lantern behind him.

Now! something inside Nick said wordlessly. Do it now!

He stepped past the grappling pair and slammed down the oak lever that released the sails of the windmill from their restraints. The roaring wind started the great shaft turning with a force and speed that doubled each second he watched. The iron chain began to coil around the spindle. In moments it had been pulled out of its spiral and lifted up from the water-filled trench in which it lay. The windmill slowed as tension increased. The chain hung in the air about four feet above the floor of the barn and extended like an arrow straight into the darkness beyond the gaping doors. Then, as the wind howled against the sails that stretched high above the roof, the iron spindle began to turn, and the clanking chain to coil around it once again.

Whatever rested beneath the black, bitter waters of the spring was being slowly raised toward the rain-lashed surface. Nick felt a brief pang of regret that he could not go out to the alders and see what emerged.

The crack of Pye's spine as it broke was like the sound of a rotten stick snapped across a knee. The Pamela-thing laughed in triumph, but before it could grasp the handle of the kerosene lantern to spill its contents across the barn, Nick snatched it up and positioned himself in the middle of the spiral trench. The Pamela-thing was no longer human. It retained only remnants of its human form. Its face was a roiling plume of black smoke that defined the vague shape of a nose and mouth. Its clutching hands were enormous tendrils of smoke so dense, its fingers resembled writhing black serpents. As Nick stared in fascination, they solidified into curved black claws, and the smoky head took on a bestial outline.

"You can't hurt me," Nick said, then repeated the words more forcefully in an attempt to convince himself. "You can't hurt me."

"That was true before, but no longer," it said in a hollow and in-human voice. "I erased the bind-rune that protected you from the circle on your bedroom floor. You are my meat now, fool."

It started toward Nick but with a hiss of frustration stepped back, baffled.

Nick remembered the notebook in the inner pocket of his jacket and drew it forth. He opened it to the page where the ritual circle with its bind-rune was drawn, and held it up for the thing to see.

"Do you mean this circle?"

It turned its eyeless face toward the lever that activated the windmill, and for a moment Nick though it would just slam up the lever and stop the turning of the sails, but it did not move from its place.

"You can't work the windmill, either, can you? And you can't touch the chain. That's why you made me hook up the rope and the tow-chain to it when you tried to drag it out with the tractor."

Nick found himself laughing hysterically and forced himself to stop. He felt more terrified than ever before in his life, but at the same time manically exhilarated. It was a stalemate.

"No, you foolish skin-bag of shit," the creature said, reading his thoughts. "I will pull this barn down around your ears."

It turned away from Nick and grasped one of the supporting posts that held up the barn's roof. The post was a foot thick, but Nick saw it flex as the creature tightened its sooty, serpentine arms. Suddenly, it cried out in pain and released the pillar. Charlie Pye was not dead, not quite. He had sunk his teeth into the black substance of the creature's leg.

The brightness of a sunrise lit up the east beyond the barn's open doors, but it was no solar event. Nick turned and saw the field and the clump of alders around the spring on its crest burning with white light. A kind of transparent bubble extended itself out from the stunted trees. The surface of the bubble danced and rippled with iridescent colours. He saw that it came no closer to the barn than the line of browned grass he had noticed in the field from the top of his ladder. Lightning ripped open the sky as the storm raged on, but so bright was this bubble of light that the flash was barely visible above it.

A sound unlike any Nick had ever heard came from the alders. It was like the rhythmic tolling of a vast bell, but much deeper in pitch so that it was almost subsonic. He felt it in his chest more than he heard it with his ears. It began to toll faster, creating with its own echoes a kind of harmonic dissonance that was also expressed in the sheets of colour that passed over the transparent bubble.

The dissonance on the air paralysed him with waves of force. He could not have turned away even had he wished to do so. He could only press the heels of his palms against his ears in a futile attempt to block out the sound. Some part of his awareness told him that the shaft of the windmill had ceased to turn, and the chain had stopped winding on the spindle and stood taunt and vibrating with tension above the field. Whatever had rested at the bottom of the spring rested there no longer.

Lines of brightness shot out from the alders in multiple directions across the ground, like the golden strands of a spider's web. Pulses of light flashed out from the trees along these strands and were answered by returning pulses. A kind of cry such as might have issued from the throat of a monstrous bird sounded from all directions. It was so loud that for an instant it drowned out the tolling of the unseen bell and the noise of the storm. Its echo died away as though borne through the night on vast wings.

Something in the windmill broke. The chain began to unravel on the spindle with an iron clanking, as whatever had been drawn up to the surface of the spring returned to its depths. The bubble of light vanished and the web of glowing lines radiating from the alders faded away. After a dozen seconds or so the chain ceased to move.

Nick took his hands away from his ears and heard a rhythmic thud on the roof of the barn. One of the sails of the windmill must have broken, and was beating against the peak as it spun unrestrained. It would beat itself to pieces if the wind did not die down soon, he thought, and turned in a kind of daze toward the Pamela-thing. It was gone. So was Charlie Pye. Nothing remained on the dirt floor of the barn to show they had ever existed.

They must have vanished with the light, he thought as he walked toward the open doors and stood watching the storm. The lightning had ceased, and the wind seemed to be falling. Maybe the worst of it was over. He looked at the dim outline of the alders on the far side of the field and thought about walking up there to see if any trace remained of what had emerged from the water. After a few seconds, he decided against it. There was a reason the house and the barn had been built so far away from the spring. Whatever resided there was dangerous in the same way an uninsulated high-tension power line was dangerous.

Had there been enough time for it to do its work before the un-ravelling chain sent it back to the depths? He peered into the sky, but without the lightning he could not see the shapes of the clouds. Charlie Pye had been sent to insure that it did its work. Sent by whom, or from where, Nick did not even try to imagine. His mind was tired. Something else had also been sent to prevent that realisa-tion, but it had failed. Had it failed? Had the windmill broken too soon?

He walked through the rain back to the house and sat in the kitchen to wait for morning.